Christopher Johnston

The Epistolary Literature of the Assyrians and Babylonians

Christopher Johnston

The Epistolary Literature of the Assyrians and Babylonians

ISBN/EAN: 9783337235673

Printed in Europe, USA, Canada, Australia, Japan

Cover: Foto ©Andreas Hilbeck / pixelio.de

More available books at **www.hansebooks.com**

THE

EPISTOLARY LITERATURE

OF THE

ASSYRIANS AND BABYLONIANS

A

DISSERTATION

PRESENTED TO THE

BOARD OF UNIVERSITY STUDIES

OF THE

JOHNS HOPKINS UNIVERSITY

FOR THE DEGREE OF

DOCTOR OF PHILOSOPHY

1894

BY

CHRISTOPHER JOHNSTON

BALTIMORE, MD.

1898

PREFACE.

The following pages are reprinted from the *Journal of the American Oriental Society*, vol. xviii, pp. 125-175, and vol. xix, pp. 41–96. For convenience of reference the original pagination has been retained. As stated in my note on p. 129 of Part I, the third and fourth volumes of Professor Robert F. Harper's *Assyrian and Babylonian Letters* appeared while the first part of my work was in press, and it was therefore impossible to make any extensive use of the material contained therein. For this reason the publication of Part II was delayed in order that I might have an opportunity to study the new volumes of Professor Harper's admirable work, and I have thus been able to make some important additions to my glossary.

The arrangement of the glossary is in accordance with the plan laid down by Professor Haupt for the preparation of the proposed Johns Hopkins Assyrian-English Glossary, and announced at the meeting of the American Oriental Society held at Baltimore, in October, 1887 (*Journ. Amer. Or. Soc.*, vol. xiii, pp. ccxliv–ccxlix; cf. *Am. Journ. of Philol.*, vol. xvii, p. 487).

I take this opportunity of expressing to Professor Haupt my sincere thanks for many valuable suggestions, for his friendly advice and encouragement given upon very many occasions, and for his kind assistance, involving no small amount of labor, in seeing these pages through the press.

CHRISTOPHER JOHNSTON,
First Lieutenant, Fifth Regiment,
I. M. N. G.

Camp Wilmer,
May, 1898.

The Epistolary Literature of the Assyrians and Babylonians.—By Dr. Christopher Johnston, Johns Hopkins University, Baltimore, Md.

While the historical, grammatical, and poetical texts bequeathed to us by the ancient peoples of Babylonia and Assyria received from the first the careful attention of Oriental scholars, the numerous tablets containing letters and dispatches have until recent years attracted only a moderate degree of interest. This was but natural. The mass of the Assyro-Babylonian literature which has come down to us is of immense extent, and the number of Assyriologists has never been large, so that a considerable degree of selection was demanded by the nature of the subject. Close study of the grammatical and lexicographical texts was absolutely necessary in order to obtain a competent knowledge of the newly discovered language. The vivid light thrown by the historical documents upon a long lost period of the world's history amply explains the zealous study bestowed upon them, while their comparatively simple style and construction rendered them a most fitting subject for workers in a new field. The many beautiful hymns and psalms discovered in the library of that great patron of letters, King Sardanapallus, and in the ruins of the Babylonian temples; the great national epic celebrating the exploits of the hero Gilgameš; the magical and liturgical texts; the intensely interesting cosmogonic legends, with the invaluable information all these supplied concerning the religion and religious myths of Western Asia, could not fail to excite deep interest in the minds of all scholars, especially when it is remembered that, at the outset, the study of Assyrian was pursued, not so much for itself, as on account of the light it was expected to shed upon the Old Testament narrative. Under these circumstances it was hardly to be expected that very great attention should be paid to a class of tablets, valuable indeed, but of minor importance compared with the texts previously mentioned, and moreover extremely difficult to interpret.

The first scholar to make use of the dispatch tablets was George Smith, who in the year 1871 published extracts from some ten of them, with transliteration and translation, in his *History of Asurbanipal.* Smith, while he often grasped the general sense of the text, was apt to be incorrect in matters of detail, and his translations are therefore faulty; but it must be borne in mind that he wrote over twenty years ago, when the field of Assyrian epistolary literature was as yet wholly unexplored. That he recognized the value of these texts is shown by his citations from them; but, having at his command abundance of material which readily yielded far more striking results, he bestowed but scant study upon them. Thus, in the section of his book devoted to the Elamite wars, he cites and translates lines 1–13 of the very important text K 13, but goes no further, although the remaining fifty-two lines would have yielded him most valuable information in regard to the subject he had in hand. During the remaining five years of his life, Smith's work was principally devoted to the exploration of the buried cities of Western Asia and to the publication of the results attained by him in this field; and, with the exception of two texts translated in his *Assyrian Discoveries*, this branch of cuneiform literature received no further attention from him.

If I am correctly informed, the German Government had requested the British Museum to furnish some translations of Assyrian letters for the Reichspost Museum of Berlin. The task was assigned to Mr. Theo. G. Pinches, who was thus obliged to devote some attention to these texts. On the 4th of December, 1877, Mr. Pinches read before the Society of Biblical Archæology a paper entitled "Notes upon the Assyrian Report Tablets, with Translation." In this paper, which was published in the Transactions of the Society for the following year (vol. vi. pp. 209–243), the author, after a general introduction, gave a summary of the contents of four letters selected by him, followed by the cuneiform text with interlinear transliteration and translation, accompanied by brief philological notes. This was the first attempt to subject the letters to systematic study on the same lines as the other branches of Assyrian literature, and it is not surprising that this pioneer work was not, in every respect, successful. It gives an idea of the difficulties surrounding the subject, that even so experienced a cuneiformist as Mr. Pinches often failed to grasp the meaning of the texts he had selected for study. But the methods of the day were in a high degree empirical. Assyrian was studied through the medium of Hebrew, Arabic, and Aramean; and a more or less happy conjecture did the rest. The present method of study, by the comparison of parallel passages and the sifting over of the whole cuneiform literature to discover the uses of each separate word, had hardly come into existence; indeed, it is to be regretted that, even to-day, a few scholars still adhere to the older and less laborious method. However, it cannot be expected that a science, which had its birth hardly fifty years ago, should in this brief time attain perfection. We should rather rejoice that so much has been accomplished than regret that so much remains to be done.

Stimulated, perhaps, by Mr. Pinches' example, one of the old pioneers of cuneiform research, the English discoverer of photography, Mr. H. Fox Talbot, next essayed to translate the very difficult text K 31. The results of his attempt appeared in the *Transactions of the Society of Biblical Archæology* for 1878, and in vol. xi. of the *Records of the Past*, published in the same year, under the title "Defense of a Magistrate falsely accused." The very title shows how completely Mr. Talbot failed to understand the text, which is an appeal for redress, made by a person who claims to have been deprived of his property and otherwise injured by personal enemies, taking advantage of certain political conditions.

Since the year 1878, Mr. Pinches has published translations of a few letters, principally in *Records of the Past;* but they must all be considered as unsuccessful attempts based on the old conjectural method of work. In justice to Mr. Pinches, however, it should be stated that, while not wholly successful in his efforts to explain these difficult texts, he has rendered most valuable services to Assyriologists in making the texts accessible. His great skill and accuracy in copying and editing cuneiform texts has been exhibited on many occasions, and he has made all students of Assyriology his debtors by his most excellent work in the preparation and revision of the second edition of the fourth volume of the *Cuneiform Inscriptions of Western Asia.*

The sketch of Assyro-Babylonian Literature in Kaulen's *Assyrien und Babylonien* (4th ed., 1891, pp. 189 ff.) contains (second hand) translations of a few letters; and both Hommel (*Geschichte Babyloniens und Assyriens*, 1885–86) and Tiele (*Babylonisch-Assyrische Geschichte*, 1886) made free use in their respective works of such letter-texts as were of historical importance.

Father J. N. Strassmaier, whose merits as a copyist are well known, published copious extracts from the letters in his *Alphabetisches Verzeichniss*, which appeared in 1886, but made no attempt at translation. In fact, until the year 1887, very little had been done toward the special study of this very interesting branch of Assyrian literature, and only a small number of complete texts had been published.[1] In 1887–89, however, an American, Mr. Samuel Alden Smith, published, in the *Proceedings of the Society of Biblical Archæology*, and in the second and third parts of his *Keilschrifttexte Asurbanipals*, sixty-nine texts copied from the best preserved letter-tablets in the British Museum, with transliteration, translation, and philological notes; Mr. Pinches, who assisted materially in editing the texts, and other cuneiformists, appended additional notes. Mr. Smith unfortunately lacked the necessary philological knowledge, and, while he added greatly

[1] Dr. C. F. Lehmann's paper, "Zwei Erlasse König Asurbanabals" (ZA. ii. 1887, pp. 58–68), in which the texts K 95 and 67, 4–2, 1 are translated, can hardly be considered as an improvement upon the work of his predecessors in the field. Dr. Lehmann, subsequently, in connection with the letters published by him in his Šamaššumukîn (1892), called attention (pp. 72–73) to the necessity for grouping all letters under the names of their respective writers, and pointed out the facilities to this end offered by Bezold's *Catalogue of the Kouyunjik Collection.* This plan has been adopted by Dr. R. F. Harper in his *Assyrian and Babylonian Letters of the K Collection*, the first volume of which appeared in that year.

to the available material for study, he did very little to elucidate the subject. His translations not only fail to reproduce the original, but are frequently so obscure as to be actually unintelligible, owing, perhaps, to his imperfect command of German.

Prof. Friedrich Delitzsch, the founder of the Leipzig school of Assyriology, who, as is evident from the numerous citations of these texts in his Assyrian Grammar and his Assyrian Dictionary, had already given much attention to the subject, next published, in the *Beiträge zur Assyriologie* (1889–91), a series of three papers on Assyrian letters, in which, unlike Smith, he gives the text in transliteration only. His commentary, however, is fuller, and he endeavors to ascertain something about the personality of the writer wherever possible. Prof. Delitzsch treated forty texts, thirty-one of which had been already translated by Smith, but in all these cases the necessity for a re-translation is obvious. Prof. Delitzsch, approaching the subject in a scientific manner, and possessing the advantages of a large experience and extensive lexicographical collections, has solved the problem, and laid down the lines upon which the study of the Assyrian epistolary literature must be carried on in the future. As in other branches of cuneiform research, he applies here the principles of common sense, even a moderate exercise of which might have saved S. A. Smith from many errors.

Perhaps the greatest difficulty in the way of a successful study of the Assyrian letters was the absence of sufficient available material upon which to work. While few, or comparatively few, texts were published, and while the great mass of those in the British Museum were not even catalogued according to their contents, the task was almost a hopeless one; but the difficulty has at last been removed. The catalogue of the Kouyunjik Collection prepared by Dr. Carl Bezold (who may be called the Chief Registrar of Assyriology), of which the first volume appeared in 1889, has rendered it possible to select these texts from the many thousands composing the collection; and an American scholar, Dr. Robert Francis Harper, of the University of Chicago, a former pupil of Delitzsch and Schrader, has been prompt to take advantage of the fact. Aided by Bezold's catalogue, Dr. Harper has within the last few years copied a large number of these texts; and a portion of the results of his labors has been given to the world in the two volumes of his *Assyrian and Babylonian Letters of the K Collection.* These two volumes, which appeared in 1892 and 1894 respectively, contain altogether two hundred and twenty-three carefully edited and excellently published letters. Many of these texts, it is true, had already been published; but their republication is necessary, owing to the plan of the author, which is to make his work a complete "Corpus Epistolarum" of the K Collection. As in the case of S. A. Smith, Mr. Pinches has again placed his great skill and experience at the disposal of the author, and has rendered valuable service in collating a large number of the texts and aiding in editing them.

For obvious reasons Dr. Harper has grouped together all the letters of each writer, and it is his purpose to publish first those texts which preserve the name of the scribe, and later those from which the name is missing. Nor does he propose to confine himself to the *K* collection, as the title of his book would indicate, but intends to publish, in the *Zeitschrift für Assyriologie* and in *Hebraica*, letters from the other collections of the British Museum, and subsequently to incorporate them in a later volume of his work. Fourteen letters of the R^m2. Collection have already appeared in volume eight of the *Zeitschrift für Assyriologie.*[1] When the texts have been published, Dr. Harper proposes to add transliterations, translations, and a glossary. (See the prefaces to Parts I. and II. of Dr. Harper's work.) It is to be hoped that this work, so excellently begun, may be carried on to successful completion.[2]

In speaking of the epistolary literature of the Assyrians reference has been had to the letters of the later period, that of the Sargonides; and, as for a long time no others were known to exist, the term has become in a manner fixed, and for the sake of convenience is retained here. Its application is now, however, no longer strictly accurate. In the winter of 1887–88 some natives found at Tel el-Amarna in Upper Egypt between three and four hundred cuneiform tablets, which proved to consist of letters and dispatches addressed to the Egyptian Court in the 15th century B. C. Of these tablets eighty-two were secured for the British Museum, and one hundred and sixty for that of Berlin; the Bûlaq Museum has sixty, and the rest are in the hands of private individuals. Excellent editions of these texts have been published by the authorities of the Berlin and British Museums, and Dr. Carl Bezold has, under the somewhat misleading title of *Oriental Diplomacy*, published in transliteration the eighty-two texts of the latter Museum, with summaries of their contents, grammatical analysis, and a glossary. While this article is going through the press, the fifth volume of Schrader's *Keilinschriftliche Bibliothek* has been issued. It contains a transliteration and translation of the Amarna texts, with glossary, indexes, etc., by Dr. Hugo Winckler, of the University of Berlin. This volume has also been published in English.

Of the literature of the subject, which has already assumed formidable proportions, a very complete bibliography is to be found in the edition of the British Museum texts published in 1892. A brief sketch of the characteristics of these interesting documents is given below (pp. 132 ff.).

---

[1] These texts have since been republished, along with numerous other new texts, in the fourth volume of Harper's work.

[2] Parts III. and IV. have just appeared, after the present article was in type. It has therefore been impossible to make any extensive use of the new material contained therein.

Under the title Assyrian letters is included a large number of documents differing greatly in contents and scope. Among them are the letters of private individuals; letters of kings to members of their families, and to various high officers of the empire; reports of governors of provinces, and of military and civil officers; proclamations; petitions; reports of priests on omens, terrestrial and celestial; astronomical reports; reports of physicians concerning patients under their care;—in short, while letters of an official character largely predominate, nearly every species of epistolary composition is represented among these interesting texts. A systematic classification of them is for the present out of the question, since Dr. Harper's book has only reached the second volume, while the information supplied by Bezold's catalogue is of the vaguest possible character and often misleading. To this is added the further difficulty, that many of those already published are as yet very obscure. In fact, no proper classification can be carried out until a much larger number of the letters has been published, and a complete concordance prepared of the names of persons and places occurring in them. The excellent plan adopted by Dr. Harper, of grouping the letters under the names of the writers, will do much to facilitate this work. When we consider the unbounded enthusiasm with which every fragment of an ancient Greek or Roman inscription is received, and remember that in these letters we possess hundreds of original contemporary documents whose authenticity is beyond all question, their value to all students of Assyro-Babylonian life and history is not easily over-estimated.

Thus, to select a few examples, the proclamation of Sardanapallus, published in IV R[2] 45, no. 1, is an urgent appeal to the Babylonians to hold aloof from the threatened revolt of his brother Šamaš-šum-ukîn,—a revolt which, when it took place, shook the Assyrian empire to its foundation and led the way to its ultimate downfall.[1] The text K 13 (IV R[2] 45, no. 2) furnishes valuable details in regard to the events which resulted in the invasion of Elam and the sacking of Susa, described in that portion of the annals of Sardanapallus recording the eighth campaign of that monarch; while the dispatch K 10 (Pinches' *Texts*, p. 6), proceeding from the same writer, affords an insight into the distracted state of the unhappy land of Elam, which, weakened by internal factional contests, fell an easy prey to the Assyrian arms.

The letters of the old courtier Rammân-šum-uçur afford a glimpse into the manners and customs of the Assyrian court in the days of the Sargonides, and two of them especially, K 183[2] and K 595 (Harper, no. 6), are models of courtly style. In the former he complains that, owing to the machinations of powerful

---

[1] See JAOS. xv. pp. 311-316; Johns Hopkins Univ. Circ., No. 106, p. 108 (June, 1893).

[2] Cf. *Beitr. zur Assyr.*, i. p. 617 ff.

enemies, his son had failed to obtain a position at court, to which, it would seem, his birth entitled him, and, with the utmost tact, appeals to the king to remedy the injustice done him; the latter letter, apparently in reply to a familiar and kindly communication from the king, contains two distinct plays upon words, by ringing the changes upon which the writer conveys a series of compliments to his royal master.

In the text K 629 (Harper, no. 65), the priest Nabû-šum-iddina outlines the program of a religious ceremony, accompanied by a procession, to be held in honor of the god Nabû at Calah, in which he proposes to take part, and concludes with a prayer for the welfare of "the prince, my lord," to whom the letter is addressed. Letters from priests, indeed, are very numerous, and usually contain answers to requests for information concerning omens, lucky or unlucky days, charms, and similar matters. It is clear, not only from the letters but also from the other branches of Assyrian literature, that it was the custom of the king to consult the will of the gods in all his undertakings, and the picture in the Book of Daniel of King Nebuchadnezzar calling in the aid of his magicians and soothsayers is by no means overdrawn.

Quite a number of the letters proceed from physicians. In one (S 1064), we find the physician Arad-Nanâ applying a bandage in a case of ophthalmia or of facial erysipelas; in K 519 he recommends plugging the anterior nares in a case of epistaxis;[1] and in K 576 he advises the king to anoint himself, to drink only pure water, and to wash his hands frequently in a bowl. From the letter K 81 we learn that when the Assyrian general Kudurru lay ill at Erech, the king sent him his own physician Iqîša-aplu, by whose efforts he was so fortunate as to be restored to health.[2]

In spite of the very complete system of laws evidenced by the contract tablets, we find petitions complaining of the subversion of justice to private ends; but too much stress should not be laid upon this. All such petitions are *ex parte* statements, and few men who lose a case at law, even at the present day, acquiesce entirely in the justice of the decision.

So many sculptures have been found representing Assyrian kings riding in chariots drawn by spirited steeds that it is interesting to find a number of dispatches reporting the arrival of horses for the use of the king, his household, or his officers; and not less interesting to learn that the most highly prized breeds of these animals were the Ethiopian and the Median, both famous among other nations of antiquity as well.[3]

These few examples will give some idea of the contents of the letters, and of what we may expect to learn from them when a sufficient amount of material has been made available. The

---

[1] See below, no. 14, S 1064.

[2] See *Beitr. zur Assyr.*, i. p. 198 ff.

[3] See *Beitr. zur Assyr.*, i. pp. 202–212; ii. pp. 44–55.

study, however, is by no means an easy one. These texts, varying in length from six or seven to sixty or seventy lines, proceed from a great variety of writers of different stations in life, and come from every part of the great Assyrian Empire. In the case of many of them we are at a loss to understand the affairs to which they refer, since they were composed under circumstances of which we have no knowledge. Events well known both to the writer and to his correspondent are frequently alluded to in such a way as to give but a slight hint, or none at all, as to their real significance. And this is to be expected, for a letter of the present day might well be totally unintelligible to one unacquainted with the writer and the person to whom it is addressed.

Dialectic peculiarities are to be expected; but here great caution must be used, since no safe conclusions can be formed upon this head with the rather scanty materials at present available. Above all, it must be borne in mind that these letters are not composed in the classical language of the historical inscriptions and the poetical texts, but in the colloquial speech of Assyria and Babylonia at the time of the Sargonides, differing from the classical language in somewhat the same way as Cicero's letters from his orations. Much, of course, depends upon the subject matter and the personality of the writer. The soldier, the priest, the physician, the astrologer, has each his technical terms and his peculiar forms of expression. But even in the most elevated epistolary style the language differs considerably from that of the historical texts. Words and forms abound which are only to be met with in this branch of cuneiform literature, and the long and flowing periods of the classical texts are here replaced by terser forms of speech. The syntactical construction is less rigid, while the employment of shorter sentences, and the frequent use of the particles, especially of the enclitic *ni*, renders the style more vivid and lively. Individual differences of style occur as a matter of course; the styles of the courtier Rammân-šum uçur and of the soldier Bel-ibnî distinctly reflect the habits and pursuits of the writers.

As stated above, the Tel el-Amarna letters are not here included under the head of Assyrian letters, a term until quite recently restricted by usage to the letters of the Sargonide period, but are treated as a special branch of cuneiform literature. They are, however, so interesting and throw so much light upon a very obscure historical period that, although not coming strictly within the scope of this paper, some brief account of them would seem to be called for.

Amenophis III., of the 18th dynasty (reigned 1413–1377 B. C.), married, as has long been known from the Egyptian monuments, a Mesopotamian princess named Tii or Thi, by whom he became the father of his successor Amenophis IV. (reigned 1376–1364 B. C.). The latter, who reigned only about twelve years, seceded from the national worship of Amen, and endeavored to substitute for it that of Aten, or the solar disk. His efforts were, however, frustrated by the vigorous opposition of the priesthood, and he retired to a place on the Nile, about a hundred and eighty miles above Memphis, where he built an entirely new temple, palace, and town. It was in the ruins of this palace, near the modern village of Tel el-Amarna, that these invaluable tablets were found in 1887–88. They consist of letters and dispatches addressed to Amenophis III., and to his son and successor Amenophis IV., by Asiatic monarchs,—among them Burnaburiaš, King of Babylon, and Ašur-uballiṭ, King of Assyria, both previously known from the cuneiform inscriptions,—and by Egyptian prefects and governors of a large number of towns in Syria and Phœnicia. All these are written in a variety of the cuneiform script intermediate between the old linear and the later cursive form, but bearing a closer affinity to the Assyrian than to the Babylonian style of writing. The language employed is, except in case of two letters, Assyrian, but, as in the letters of a later period, it differs considerably from that of the historical inscriptions. The dispatches from Syria and Phœnicia, moreover, exhibit a number of peculiarities due to the influence of Canaanite environment, and in some cases genuine Canaanite words are added as explanatory glosses to Assyrian phrases.[1] One of the letters is composed in the language of Mitani, and another in that of Arçapi, of which no specimens had previously been discovered.

The letters from the more distant Asiatic princes are uniformly friendly in tone, and refer to treaties with Egypt, to mutual alliances by marriage, to commercial relations, and to the interchange of gifts. With the close, apparently, of the reign of Amenophis III. begins a series of letters and dispatches from Syria and Phœnicia indicating the decadence of the Egyptian power in those countries. Revolt after revolt is reported, and the aid of more troops is constantly demanded. The cities are all falling away from the king; the friends of Egypt are few and weak, and surrounded by powerful enemies; unless promptly supported by strong reinforcements they can no longer hold out, and the whole country must soon be lost to the Egyptian monarch.

Most of these tablets are to be referred to the troubled reign of Amenophis IV., who, weakened by his unsuccessful contest with the priesthood of the old religion, was unable to keep in subjection his Syrian vassals, while the latter were prompt to take advantage of his weakness in order to achieve their independence. It is a most interesting fact that five of these letters are from Jerusalem, which thus appears as a city of importance even in the days before the Exodus. An excellent translation of the Jerusalem letters is given by Dr. H. Zimmern in the *Zeitschrift für Assyriologie*, vi. pp. 245–263.

---

[1] See Zimmern, *Zeitschrift für Assyriologie*, vi. p. 154; and cf. *The Tel el-Amarna Tablets in the British Museum*, 1892, pp. xiii, xiv, of the Introduction, from which the facts given above are chiefly derived.

The Tel el-Amarna letters have attracted so much attention, and so much has been written about them (see the excellent bibliography appended to the British Museum edition), that further discussion is unnecessary in a paper not specially devoted to the subject. The field, however, is by no means exhausted. While the general contents of these valuable and interesting documents is pretty well known, only a comparatively small number of them has as yet been translated in a satisfactory manner, and the recent discovery of a cuneiform tablet of the same period at Tel el-Hesy, the site of the ancient Lachish,[1] gives fair promise that at no distant day the treasure may receive material additions.

In the following section, twenty selected letters are presented in transliteration, with translations and explanatory introductions. Seven of them, viz. Nos. 1, 2 (ll. 1–13), 4, 5, 6, 14, and 16, have already been translated, as will be found noted in each case; but they are here newly treated, and the present translations are offered as substitutes for those which have previously appeared. The rest are here translated for the first time. In all cases the writer has endeavored to render the Assyrian texts into intelligible English, without, however, departing from the sense and spirit of the original.

The accompanying transliterations are an attempt to embody the views of the writer as to the grammatical reconstruction of the Assyrian text; such explanations as may seem necessary will be given in the philological notes in Part II., which will also contain syllabic transliterations and literal translations.

Part I. has been prepared with special reference to non-Assyriologists, and therefore all matter of an exclusively technical nature has been reserved for Part II.

PART I.

Selected Letters, Transliterated and Translated.

1.

K 524.

Among the numerous Assyrian and Babylonian letters which have been preserved, none are more interesting than those of a certain Bel-ibnî. Rich in historical allusions, they cast a most valuable side-light upon the actors and events of an important period, and furnish many suggestive details. Seven of these letters have already been published, and, in the preface to the second part of his *Assyrian and Babylonian Letters of the K Collection*, Prof. R. F. Harper promises to edit the whole series

---

[1] See *Recueil des Travaux*, xv. p. 137; *Quarterly Statement of the Palestine Exploration Fund*, Jan. 1893, pp. 25 ff.

in the third part of that valuable work.[1] Three letters from King Sardanapallus to Bel-ibnî have also been published with transliteration, translation, and commentary, and his name is mentioned in a number of other letters of the period.

Bel-ibnî was a man of high rank, a general in the armies of Sardanapallus, and served with distinction during the revolt of Šumaš-šum-ukîn and in the campaigns against Elam and the war-like Chaldeans of Southern Babylonia. As to his birth and family relations, we have little information. He had, however, a brother, Belšunu, and a nephew, his sister's son, Mušezib-Marduk. The nephew held a high military command under Bel-ibnî; Belšunu, seized by Nabû-bel-šumâte at the time of his revolt, was thrown into prison, loaded with chains, and held in captivity for a considerable period—an injury which goes far to account for the implacable animosity exhibited by Bel-ibnî towards the Chaldean prince. Bel-ibnî himself, according to a proclamation of the King to the people of the Gulf District, held the rank of *manzaz pâni*, a dignity reserved for the most exalted nobility and the highest officers of state, the possessors of which, as the name implies, enjoyed the right of access to the royal presence and of a place near the King's person on all occasions of ceremony.

All the letters which passed between the King and Bel-ibnî are marked, says Prof. Delitzsch (*B. A.*, i. p. 234), by the most cordial good feeling. Those addressed by the monarch to his general may be called almost affectionate in tone, and in one instance, when it seemed necessary to administer a reproof for an apparent disregard of instructions, the sting is removed by a prompt forgiveness and an expression of the utmost confidence. A translation of this letter by the present writer will be found in *Jour. Amer. Orient. Soc.*, xv. pp. 313, 314. The letters of Bel-ibnî to his sovereign, while exhibiting all the respect due to the royal station and preserving all the forms of Oriental etiquette, are yet characterized by a certain soldier-like frankness and directness of speech; and stamp the writer as a man earnest and capable in the discharge of his duties, self-reliant and thoroughly practical in all emergencies, and conscious that he both enjoyed and deserved the confidence of his friend and master.

In the year 652 B. C. (Tiele, *Babyl. Assyr. Geschichte*, p. 377), Kudurru, Governor of Erech, reports to the King that he has received a message from Sin-tabnî-uçur, Governor of Ur, stating that he has been summoned by Šamaš-šum-ukîn, King of Babylon and brother of Sardanapallus, to join in his revolt against Assyria, and praying earnestly for reinforcements, which he (Kudurru) has forthwith despatched (K 5457). In this letter Bel-ibnî is mentioned, but it is impossible to make out the con-

[1] The third volume, just issued, contains seven letters of Bel-ibnî, including a new one (K 597), hitherto unpublished. Harper has failed to see that K 1250 and K 1374 (see below, p. 136) belong to the same group.

text owing to the mutilation of the tablet. The text is published in Winckler's *Sammlung von Keilschrifttexten*, ii. p. 55.

In the year 650 B. C. (Tiele, *op. cit.*, p. 381), Bel-ibnî was appointed governor of the *Mât Tâmti*^m, the district lying along the Persian Gulf (K 812; S. A. Smith, *Asurb.*, ii. p. 49), and in the same year writes to the King that he has forwarded to the Assyrian court Tammaritu, the fugitive King of Elam, recently deposed by Indabigaš, together with his family and adherents who shared his flight (K 599; Smith, *Asurb.*, p. 196).

In the letter K 5062 (Winckler, *op. cit.*, ii. p. 69), which is unfortunately so mutilated as to yield no connected sense, he mentions Tammaritu (obv. ll. 15, 17, 27, 30) and Nabû-bel-šumâte (obv. l. 31). The text K 1250 (Winckler, *op. cit.*, ii. p. 59) is badly mutilated at the beginning and end, and the name of the writer is broken away; its matter and style, however, together with a number of peculiar forms of expression, stamp it unmistakably as the composition of Bel-ibnî. A comparison of this text with K 13 leaves no doubt upon the subject.[1] "Before the troops of the lord of kings, my lord," he writes, "terror has entered (into Elam) like a ravaging disease" (ll. 8–10). "When the troops of the lord of kings, my lord, enter Dûr-ili . . . . . they shall seize that vile wretch, accursed of the gods, Nabû-bel-šumâte, and the villains who are with him, give them to the lord of kings, my lord, release all the Assyrians he holds captive, and send him to the lord of kings, my lord. When that vile wretch, accursed of the gods, Nabû-bel-šumâte, revolted some four years ago, he bound with fetters, hand (literally 'side') and foot, Belšunu, my eldest brother, a servant of the lord of kings, my lord, (and) cast him into prison" (ll. 11–25).

A Belšunu, Governor of Khindana, was eponym about the year 648 B. C. (Tiele, p. 389), but whether he was the brother of Bel-ibnî is uncertain. If the revolt of Nabû-bel-šumâte be correctly placed in 651 B. C. (Tiele, p. 381), this letter must have been written in the year 647.

Like the preceding text, K 1374 (Winckler's *Sammlung von Keilschrifttexten*, ii. pp. 20, 21) is badly mutilated, and the name of the writer is broken off. But a comparison of what remains of the introduction with other letters of Bel-ibnî clearly shows that this text proceeds from the same writer. We find also (obv. ll. 1, 8; rev. ll. 15, 18, 20, 21, 25) the king referred to as "lord of kings, my lord," an expression peculiar to the style of Bel-ibnî. He states (obv. ll. 17, 18) that all Elam has revolted against King Ummakhaldas (Ummanaldas);[2] mentions, among other persons, Umkhulumâ (rev. l. 3) and Nabû-bel-šumâte (rev. l. 6);

---

[1] Compare, e. g. K 1250, 8–10 with K 13, 16–18; K 1250, 11–16 with K 13, 41–43. Note also the epithet *sikipti Bel* applied to Nabû-bel-šumâte, K 1250, 14, 22–3; K 13, 39, and the use of the expression *bel šarrâni, beliia*, which characterizes all the letters of Bel-ibnî.

[2] This may refer to the rebellion of Umbakhabû'a mentioned *Asurb.*, v. 16–17.

and refers to the messengers of Šamaš-šum-ukîn, the rebellious brother of Sardanapallus (rev. l. 7). Towards the close of the letter (rev. ll. 17 ff.) he complains that though he has several times applied for horses, which are very much needed, he has been unable to obtain them.

The following letter from Bel-ibnî to the king (K 524) is published, with transliteration, translation, and commentary, in S. A. Smith's *Keilschrifttexte Asurbanipals*, ii. pp. 54–58, to which are appended additional notes and corrections by Pinches (pp. 78–78), and by Strassmaier (pp. 87–88). Those points in which the translation offered below differs from that of Smith and his learned collaborators will be noticed in the philological notes.

The account given of the dealings of Nadân with Nabû-bel-šumâte, and the recommendation of summary punishment in case of any attempt to continue the intercourse, would seem to indicate that the revolt of the Chaldean prince had already been effected; while the flight from Elam of Šumâ, the nephew of Tammaritu, points to the brief reign of Indabigaš. It is probable that Šumâ, unable, perhaps on account of the illness referred to in the letter, to accompany his uncle when the latter, deposed by Indabigaš, escaped to Babylonia, made his way to the border as best he could, and was received by Bel-ibnî as related in the letter, which, if this conjecture be correct, should be referred to the year 650 B. C. The text may be translated as follows :

TRANSLATION.

To the lord of kings, my lord, thy servant Bel-ibnî! May Ašur, Šamaš, and Marduk decree length of days, health of mind and body, for the lord of kings, my lord!

Šumâ, the son of Šum-iddina, son of Gakhal—son of Tammaritu's sister—fleeing from Elam, reached the (country of the) Dakkhâ. I took him under my protection and transferred him from the Dakkhâ (hither). He is ill. As soon as he completely recovers his health, I shall send him to the king, my lord.

A messenger has come to him (with the news) that Nadân and the Pukudeans of Til. . . .[1] had a meeting with Nabû-bel-šumâte at the city of Targibâti, and they took a mutual oath to this effect: "According to agreement we shall send you whatever news we may hear." To bind the bargain(?) they purchased from him fifty head of cattle, and also said to him: "Our sheep shall come and graze in the pasture(?), among the Ubanateans, in order that you may have confidence in us." Now (I should advise that) a messenger of my lord the king come, and give Nadân plainly to understand as follows: If thou sendest anything to Elam for sale, or if a single sheep gets over to the Elamite pasture (?), I will not let thee live." The king my lord may thoroughly rely upon my report.

---

[1] Apparently a compound name like Til-Khumba; cf. Delitzsch, *Paradies*, pp. 323, 325.

ACCENTED TRANSLITERATION.

[1]*Ana bel šarrâni beli̯a* [2]*ardûka Bel-ibnî!*

[3]*Ašur, Šamaš, u Marduk* [4]*ardâku ûme ṭâb libbi*[5] *u ṭâb šîri ša bel šarrâni* [6]*beli̯a liqbû!*

Šumâ [7]*mârušu ša Šum-iddina, mâr Gaxal—*[8]*mâr axâtišu ša Tammariti—*[9]*ultu mât Elamti kî* [10]*ixliqu adî Daxxa'* [11]*ittalka. Ultu Daxxa'* [12]*qâtsu kî açbata,* [13]*ultebirâšu.*

Maruç. [14]*Adî zîmešu malâ* [15]*içâbatu, ana šarri* [16]*beli̯a ašaparâšu.* [17]*Apil šipri ibâšu ša Nadân* [18]*u Puqûdu,* (Rev.) [19]*ša ina âl Til*[....], [20]*ana pân Nabû-bel-šumâte* [21]*ana âl Targibâti ittalkû.* [22]*Šumu ili ana axâmeš* [23]*ultelû, umma: "Kî adî* [24]*ṭemu mala nišemû,* [25]*nišaparâka." U, ana* [26]*idatûtu, alpe* I. KU [27]*ana kaspi ina qâtišu itabkûni.* [28]*U iqtabûni-šu umma:* [29]*"Immereni lillikûni-ma,* [30]*ina libbi.* [30a]*Uba'ânat* [31]*ina šâdu lîkulû, ina libbi* [32]*ana muxxini tarûxuç."*

[33]*Ennâ! Apil šipri ša šarri beli̯a* [34]*lillikû-ma, ina birit* [35]*îni ša Nadân lûmandid* [36]*umma: "Kî manma ana maxîri* [37]*ana mât Elamti taltapra,* [38]*u išten immeru* [39]*ana šâdu ša mât Elamti* [40]*ipterku,* (Edge) [41]*ul uballaṭka."*

Dibbe ka'âmânûtu [42]*ana šarri beli̯a altapra.*

2.

K 13.

This letter is published in Assyrian transcription in the first edition of *The Cuneiform Inscriptions of Western Asia*, vol. iv (pl. 52, no. 2), and in the original cursive Babylonian character in the second edition of that work (pl. 45, no. 2). Lines 1–13 are published with transliteration and translation in George Smith's *History of Assurbanipal*, pp. 197 ff.

The situation would seem to have been as follows: Tammaritu, king of Elam, having been dethroned in the year 650 B. C. by Indabigaš, who made himself king in his stead, made his escape to the coast of the Persian Gulf, accompanied by his family and adherents, among whom were included many high officers of state. Embarking there, he reached the Babylonian shore, whence the whole party was forwarded to the Assyrian court by Bel-ibnî, who had been recently appointed governor of the Gulf District. (See above, p. 137.) On being admitted to an audience with the Assyrian monarch, Tammaritu humiliated himself before him, and besought his aid in recovering his lost kingdom. (Tiele, pp. 380, 381.) In the meantime Nabû-bel-šumâte, grandson of the Chaldean king of Babylon, Merodach-baladan, had thrown off the authority of Assyria and withdrawn to Elam, taking with him as captives certain Assyrians who had been detailed, ostensibly to aid in the defense of his dominions, but in reality, doubtless, to protect Assyrian interests there. Sardanapallus demanded the release of the prisoners and the surrender of Nabû-bel-šumâte, the perpetrator of the outrage, threatening, in case of a refusal to comply with his demand, to invade Elam, depose Indabigaš, and place Tammaritu on the throne. Before this message reached its destination, however, the Elamite monarch had been deposed by a revolution, and Ummanaldaš made king in his stead (*Ašurb.*, iv. 114, 115; Cyl. B. vii. 71–87; Cyl. C. vii. 88–115; *K. B.*, ii. pp. 266 ff.). The latter would seem, according to our report (ll. 23–31), to have been inclined to accept the terms of the king of Assyria, but to have lacked the power. Elam was accordingly invaded, and Ummanaldaš, unable to make effective resistance, abandoned his capital, Madâktu, and took refuge in the mountains, leaving the way clear for his rival Tammaritu, who was, with little or no resistance, established on the throne as a vassal of Assyria (*Ašurb.*, iv. 110–v. 22). But the new king, proving ungrateful and rebellious, was soon deposed; Elam was again invaded; and the troops of Sardanapallus, after ravaging the country, returned home laden with spoil (*Ašurb.*, v. 23–62). Ummanaldaš now quietly resumed his kingdom, but was not long allowed to remain undisturbed. Sardanapallus again made preparation for an invasion, and Ummanaldaš, on the approach of the invading forces, once more left Madâktu, and endeavored to make head against his enemies in the regions beyond the river Id'id'e (*Ašurb.*, v. 66–75). It is to this juncture of affairs that the report refers. It may be translated as follows:

Translation.

To the lord of kings, my lord, thy servant Bel-ibnî! May Ašur, Šamaš, and Marduk grant health of mind and body, long life, and a lengthy reign to the lord of kings, my lord!

The news from Elam is as follows: Ummakhaldaš, the former king, who fled, but returned again and seated himself upon the throne, has become alarmed and left the city of Madâktu. His mother, his wife, his sons, and all his family having removed, he crossed the river Ulæus, and went southward (?) to Talakh. The *Nâgir* Ummansimaš, Undadu the *Zilliru*, and all his partisans have gone in the direction of Šukharisungur, now saying: "We will dwell in the Khukhan country," and now again "in Kha'âdâlu."[1]

All these parts are in terror; for the troops of the lord of kings, my lord, have brought panic into Elam, and spread abroad calamity like a plague. When need came upon their land, the whole country fell away from their side. All the Dakkhadeans and the Sallukkeans are in

[1] In their irresolution they were unable to form a decided and consistent plan.

a state of revolt, saying: "Why did ye slay Umkhulumâ?" When Ummakhaldaš entered Madâktu, calling together all his partisans, he upbraided them as follows: "Did I not say to you before I fled that I wished to seize Nabû-bel-šumâte and give him up to the king of Assyria, in order that he might not send his troops against us? You heard me, and can bear witness to my words."

Now, if it please the lord of kings, my lord, let me (privately) convey the royal signet to Ummakhaldaš, with reference to the capture of Nabû-bel-šumâte. I shall send it to Ummakhaldaš as a guarantee (?). If my lord the king should think, They are .... I shall send my message to them for a guarantee (?), (I would suggest that) when the royal messenger reaches them accompanied by an escort of troops, that accursed scoundrel Nabû-bel-šumâte will hear of it, and, paying a ransom to the nobles, will buy himself off. If the gods of the lord of kings, my lord, would only bestir themselves, they would catch him with his bow unstrung, and send him to the lord of kings, my lord.

They collect all the tax corn (?) in Elam, and, putting it in charge of the *šarnuppu*,[1] they live on it. As long as Umkhulumâ was alive, Nabû-bel-šumâte, on receiving his share, would lavish it upon his partisans. This tax corn (?), in charge of the *šarnuppu*, they levy from Talakh as far as Radê, and throughout the country of Salluk. Now, Nabû-bel-šumâte, and Niskhur-bel, his major-domo, whenever they catch a *šarnuppu*, seize him, saying: "Whenever you applied to Umkhulumâ for our provisions, he used to give them to you. You have slain the people of our house with famine. You shall straightway restore to us our stolen provisions, at the rate of ten *bar* for one *qa*." (?) They withhold it from Ummakhaldaš, and, though he has applied (?) for it repeatedly, he cannot get it from them. Whenever I hear anything which the lord of kings, my lord, would wish to hear, ...

The few remaining lines are too badly mutilated for translation.

ACCENTED TRANSLITERATION.

[1][*Ana bel šarrâni, beli*]*i̯a, ardúka Bel-ibnî!*

[2][*Ašur, Šamaš, u Marduk*] *ṭûbi libbi, ṭûbi šîri,* [3][*ardâku ûme*], *labâr pale ana bel šarrâni,* [4]*beli̯a, liqîšû! Ṭemu ša mât Elamti:*

[5]*Ummaxaldâšu, šarru maxrû ša ixliqa* [6]*itûrá-ma ina kussî ûšíbu,* [7]*kî iplaxu, âl Madâkti undéšer.* [8]*Ummušu, aššatsu, mâréšu, u qinnášu gabbi* [9]*kî ikmisû, nâr Ulâ'a, ana šupâl šâru,* [10]*etébir, ana âl Talux ittalka. Nâgiru* [11]*Ummanšimaš, Undadu zilliru,* [12]*u bel ṭâbâtešu, mala ibášû,* [13]*ittalkû pânišunu ana âl Šuxarisungur* [14]*šuknû. Iqábû ummakî: "Ina Xuxân,"* [15]*u kî "Ina âl Xa'âdâlu nuššab."*

---

[1] An Elamite official title.

[16]*Agâ gabbi ina puluxti, ša emûqu ša bel* [17]*šarrâni beli̯a mât Elamti kîma de'i xurruru* [18]*maruští iparrû, puluxti ulteribû;* [19]*u, itti sunqu ina mâtišunu ittaškin,* [20]*mâtsunu gabbi ina kutallišunu muššurat.* [21]*Daxxadi'û'â, Sallukki'â gabbi* [22]*sixû šunûtu, umma: "Minâ-ma Umxulumâ'* [23]*tadûkâ."*

Ûmu ša Ummaxaldâšu ana âl Madâktu [24]*erubu, bel ṭâbâtešu gabbi kî upaxxir,* [25]*dîni ittišunu iddébub, umma:* [26]*"Ul agâ'a amât ša, adî lâ axáliqu,* [27]*aqbâkunûšu, umma: "Nabû-bel-šumâte* [28]*luçbat-ma, ana šar mât Aššur luddin,* [29]*emûqešu ana muxxîni lâ išápar?—*[30]*Ta(?)tašmâ'inni, ina muxxi amâti̯a* [31]*tattašizzâ'." Ennâ! kî* [32]*pân bel šarrâni, beli̯a, maxru, unqu šarri* [33]*ana muxxi çabâta Nabû-bel-šumâte* [34]*ana pân Ummaxaldâšu lušebiluní-ma.* [35]*Anâku paširâti ana Ummaxaldâšu* [36]*lušebilšu. Nindema šarru beli̯a iqâbî umma:* [37]*"Šunu tullummâ'u: šipirtâ paširâti* [38]*ana pânišunu ašápar." Kî apil šipri ša šarri beli̯a, ina qât dîkîtu,* [39]*ana pânišunu ittalka, sikipti Bel Nabû-bel-šumâte* [40]*išémî-ma, tapšuru ana rubešu igámar-ma,* [41]*râmánšu iṭṭer. Nindema ilâni ša bel šarrâni, beli̯a,* [42]*ippušû-ma, ina qašti ramîti içabatû-ma, ana* [43]*bel šarrâni, beli̯a, išáparûni-šu.*

Še' šibši [44]*ša mât Elamti gabbi upaxxarû-ma, ana parâsu* [45]*ša šarnuppu inamdinû ina libbi balṭû.* [46]*Ultu Umxulumâ' balṭu, Nabû-bel-šumâte,* [47]*bâbšu kî içbatu, ana bel ṭâbâtešu iddur.* [48]*Še' agâ ša šibši, parâsu ša šarnuppu,* [49]*ultu âl Talax adî âl Rade u* [50]*Sallukki'â gabbi ittanaššû.* [51]*Ennâ! Šarnuppi gabbi kî ilmûni,* [52]*Nabû-bel-šumâte u Nisxur-Bel rab bîtišu* [53]*içabtû, umma: "Ana muxxi kurummâtini ana* [54]*Umxalumâ' kî tuše'idâ, kurummâtani* [55]*iddanakunûšu; Nîše bîtini ina bâbâtâ* [56]*tadûkâ. Ennâ! ana* I. QA. A. AN. X. BAR. A. AN. [57]*kurûmâtani ša mašâ' tamáxarâní-ma* [58]*tanamdinânâšu." Itti Ummaxaldâšu* [59]*ušazzûšu;* II-*šu* III-*šu kî uše'iduš,* [60]*ina qâtišunu ul iṭeršu.*

Kî amât ša ana çibûtu [61]*bel šarrâni, beli̯a, axtassu, ul kirbiku-ma* [62] .... *ul ušašmû. Kalbi râ'imu* [63] .... *mala tallaka ana ekalli* [64] .... *bel šarrâni, beli̯a ana* [65] .... *lâ išákan.*

The fate of Nabû-bel-šumâte is known to us from the historical inscriptions. Shortly after the events narrated above, Elam was overrun by the Assyrian troops, its ancient capital Susa was captured and sacked, and, driven at length to despair, the gallant Chaldean and his armor-bearer slew each other to avoid falling alive into the hands of the implacable Assyrian monarch. Ummanaldaš, who had taken refuge in the mountains, sent the body of the rebel to Sardanapallus, who satisfied his vengeance by heaping insults upon the corpse of his life-long enemy (*Ašurb.*, vii. 16–50). Thus ended the line of Merodach-baladan, which for three generations had offered a stubborn resistance to the might of the Assyrian empire.

3.

K 10.

Bel-ibnî's nephew Mušêzib-Marduk seems to have been regarded with special favor by King Sardanapallus, and, though nowhere qualified as *manzaz pâni*, had, as we are informed in a letter from the king to his general, always been honored with ready admission to the monarch's presence (*B. A.*, i. p. 236, ll. 7, 8). Kudurru, the loyal governor of Erech, thus refers to him in a letter to the king: "Mušêzib-Marduk, sister's son of Bel-ibnî, who has several times presented himself before my lord the king on errands of Bel-ibnî, has been entrusted with (this affair) by Bel-ibnî. The officers in charge of the gates inform him that these people are not well disposed towards my lord's house, and that it will not be well to let them come over here. They will give information to Elam in regard to the country of my lord the king; and in case a famine should occur in Elam, will supply provisions there" (K 1066, Winckler's *Sammlung von Keilschrifttexten*, ii. p. 38, ll. 20–30). Unfortunately, the name of the people about whom Mušêzib-Marduk thus reports is broken away, but they must have been a tribe living on Elamite territory near the Assyrian border.

The following letter, K 10, is published in Pinches' *Texts in the Babylonian Wedge-Writing*, p. 6, and contains a report from Bel-ibnî to the king concerning a successful raid into Elam under command of Mušêzib-Marduk.[1] Lines 15–25 of the reverse, conveying the latest news received from Elam, are published with transliteration and translation in George Smith's *History of Assurbanipal*, p. 248. Smith (p. 254) was inclined to identify Ummanigaš son of Amedirra with Ummanigaš son of Umbadara, whose statue was conveyed to Assyria by Sardanapallus at the time of the sacking of Susa (*Ašurb.*, vi. 52); but this is hardly possible. The royal images removed from Susa would seem rather to have been those of the more ancient kings of Elam, and it is much more likely that Ummanigaš son of Umbadara was the monarch who, according to the Babylonian Chronicle (i. 9), ascended the throne in the year 742 B. C.

Tiele's conjecture (*Babyl.-Assyr. Geschichte*, p. 399, n. 1) is much more probable. After the overthrow of Elam and the sacking of Susa, Ummanaldaš continued for some time to rule

---

[1] Cf. Delitzsch, *Kossäer*, p. 46.

over his shattered kingdom, until finally, overthrown by a revolution, he was captured by the successful rebels, sent to Assyria, and handed over to Sardanapallus, who treated him in a most humiliating manner. Along with other captive princes, he was harnessed to a car, and forced to draw it through the streets of Nineveh in the triumphal procession of his conqueror (*Ašurb.*, x. 6 ff.). This revolution, so disastrous for the unfortunate Ummanaldaš, Tiele is inclined to identify with the revolt of Ummanigaš son of Amedirra, mentioned in the present text. It is entirely possible, however, that some other rebellion, not mentioned in the historical inscriptions, is here recorded. The text may be translated as follows:

TRANSLATION.

To the lord of kings, my lord, thy servant Bel-ibnî!

May Ašur, Šamaš, and Marduk bestow health of mind, health of body, length of days, long years of reign, upon the lord of kings, the king of the world, my lord!

When I left the Gulf District, I sent five hundred soldiers, servants of my lord the king, to the city of Sabdânu, with these orders: "Establish a post (?) in Sabdânu, and make raids into Elam; slay and take prisoners!" When they reached the city of Irgidu, a city lying two leagues this side of Susa, they slew Ammaladin,[1] Prince of Iaši'an,[2] his two brothers, three of his uncles, two of his nephews, Dalân son of Adiadî'a, and two hundred free-born citizens—they had a long journey before them—and made one hundred and fifty prisoners. The authorities of Lakhiru and the people of Nugû', when they saw that my troops had got to their rear, becoming alarmed, sent a message, and entered into terms with Mušêzib-Marduk, my sister's son, a servant of my lord the king, whom I had placed in command of the post (?), saying: "We will become subjects of the king of Assyria." So, assembling all their force, they marched with Mušêzib-Marduk into Elam ....[3] They bring (?) the following report from Elam. Ummanigaš son of Amedirra has revolted against Ummakhaldaš. From the river Khudkhud as far as the city of Kha'âdânu the people have sided with him. Ummakhaldaš has assembled his forces, and now they are encamped opposite each other on the banks of the river. Iqîša-aplu, whom I have sent to the palace, is well informed about them. Let him be questioned at the palace.

---

[1] This name recalls Ammuladi(n), sheikh of the Kedarenes, who was conquered by Sardanapallus in his campaign against Arabia (*Ašurb.*, viii. 15).

[2] For the name of this district, cf. Delitzsch, *Kossäer*, p. 47, n. 1. In the Prism-inscription of Sennacherib (col. v. l. 32), the region is called *Ias'an*, Assyrian *s* representing foreign *š*.

[3] The text is here too badly mutilated for translation.

ACCENTED TRANSLITERATION.

[1]*Ana bel šarrâni, belii̯a, ardúka* [2]*Bel-ibnî!*

Ašur, Šamaš, u Marduk ṭûbi libbi, [3]*ṭûbi šîri, arâku ûme, u labâr* [4]*pale ana bel šarrâni, šar mâtâti, belii̯a* [5]*liqîšû!*

Ûmu ša ultu mât Tâmti[m] [6]*uçâ'* VC *çâbe, ardâni ša šarri belii̯a,* [7]*ana âl Çabdânu altapra, umma:* [8]"*Kâdu ina âl Çabdânu uçrâ, u* [9]*tibânu ina mât Elamti tebâ'.* [10]*dîkti dûkâ u xubtu* [11]*xubtânu.*" *Ana muxxi âl Irgidu*—[12]*âlu šû* II *kasbu qaqqar ana axû agâ* [13]*šâ âl Šušân—kî itbû, Ammaladin* [14]*nasîku ša Iâši'ân,* II *axešu,* [15]III *axe abišu,* II *mâre axišu, Dalân* [16]*mâr Adi̯adî'a, u* IIC *mâre-banûti* [17]*ša âli idûkû—qaqqar ina pânišunu* [18]*râqu—xubte* CL [19]*ixtabtûni. Nasîkâti* [20]*šâ âl Laxiru u Nugû',* [21]*ultu muxxi ša emurû-ma* [22]*xii̯âlânii̯a ana axišunu* [23]*ullî ittenîbû* [24]*kî iplaxû, pîšunu* [25]*iddánûnu, ade itti* (Rev.) [1]*Mušezib-Marduk mâr axtâii̯a, ardu ša* [*šarri*] [2]*belii̯a, ša ina muxxi kâ*[*du*] [3]*apqidu, iççabtû umma:* "*Ard*[*âni*] [4]*šu šar mât Aššur anîni.*" *qaštašunu* [5]*mala ibášû kî idkû,* [6]*itti Mušezib-Marduk . . . . a-ni,* [7]*ina mât Elamti it*[*bûni*] . . . . . *u,* [8]*qâtšunu ana lib*[*bi . . . .*] MEŠ-*šunu* [9]*ittadû . . . . tišunu,* [10]*ša ina qât Iqîša-aplu . . . . .* [*Mušezib*]-*Marduk,* [11]*ardu ša šarri beli*[*i̯a . . . .*]*ni* [12]*ina muxxi kâ*[*du*] . . . . [13]*iqridánu . . . . . . ti,* [14]*ša usebilû*[*ni* (?)*ana šarri belii̯a*(?)*al*]*tapra.*

[15]*Ṭemu ša mât Elamti iqá*(?)*bû-ma* [16]*umma:—*

Ummanigaš apil Amedirra [17]*sîxu ana muxxi Ummaxaldâšu* [18]*etépuš. Ultu nâr Xudxud* [19]*adî âl Xa'âdânu ittišu* [20]*ittašizzû. Ummaxaldâšu,* [21]*emûqešu kî upaxxir,* [22]*adû ina muxxi nâri ana tarçi* [23]*axameš nadû.*

Iqîša-aplu, [24]*ša ana Ekalli ašpura, ṭenšunu* [25]*xariç. Ina ekalli liš'alšu.*

4.

K 528.

Urtaku, King of Elam, who ascended the throne in the year 675 B. C., maintained friendly relations with Assyria during the lifetime of Esarhaddon; and the latter's son and successor, Sardanapallus, endeavored to preserve this state of affairs. When a famine broke out in Elam, the Assyrian monarch sent grain for the relief of the distressed people, protected those Elamites who had taken refuge on Assyrian territory, and restored them to their country when the long drought was over and the land was once more productive (*K. B.*, ii. p. 244). But Chaldean influence, ever hostile to Assyria, had become powerful at the court of Susa.

Urtaku allowed himself to be swayed by it, and, apparently without warning, marched against Babylon. Sardanapallus, though taken by surprise, lost no time in marching to the relief of the threatened city, signally defeated Urtaku, and compelled him to retire to Elam, where he soon after died. Among the Chaldeans who took part in this affair was Bel-iqîša, prince of Gambûlu, a marshy district of southeastern Babylonia about the mouth of the river Uknû, the modern Karoon,[1] and bordering upon Elam. Bel-iqîša, who was an Assyrian subject, cast off his allegiance, and, crossing over into Elam, joined Urtaku and took part in his ill-fated expedition. In the following year he was accidentally killed (*K. B.*, ii. p. 244, ll. 56–58). His son and successor, Dunânu, bitterly hostile to Assyria, allied himself with Teumman, the successor of Urtaku, and on the defeat and death of his Elamite ally, his land was ravaged, its inhabitants put to the sword, and he himself with all his family carried captive to Assyria. Here he was forced to take part in the conqueror's triumphal entry into Nineveh, with the head of the slain Teumman hanging to his neck, and was finally put to death with frightful tortures (*Ašurb.*, iv. 50 ff.; *K. B.*, ii. pp. 254–256).

Nabû-ušabšî, the writer of the two letters translated below, was an Assyrian official of Erech in Southern Babylonia. He seems to have suffered severely from the revolt of Bel-iqîša, and his advice in regard to the reduction of Gambûlu was doubtless in full accord with his personal feelings, which, indeed, he is at no pains to conceal. His letter which is published in *The Cuneiform Inscriptions of Western Asia*, vol. iv., pl. 47, no. 2 (2d ed.), may be translated as follows:[2]

TRANSLATION.

To the king of the world, my lord, thy servant Nabû-ušabšî!

May Erech and E-anna bless the king of the world, my lord! I pray daily to Ištar of Erech and to Nanâ for the life of the king, my lord.

The king, my lord, has sent me (this message): "Put troops on the march, and send them against Gambûlu." (Now) the gods of the king, my lord, know well that since Bel-iqîša revolted from my lord the king, and went to Elam, destroyed my father's house, and came to slay my brother, daily[3] . . . . . . With regard to what the king, my lord, has

---

[1] See Haupt, Johns Hopkins University Circulars, No. 114, p. 111b. The river of Balakhshân referred to by Ibn Batûtah in the passage quoted by Prof. Haupt is, according to Haupt, the Koktcha (i. e. "Blue River," كوك چاى), a tributary of the Oxus (Amoo-Darya).

[2] This text is also published, with transliteration, translation, and notes, by Pinches in *TSBA.*, vi. pp. 228 ff.

[3] For the next five lines the text is almost entirely obliterated, but probably contained the statement that the writer prays daily for revenge upon those who have thus injured him.

sent (to command), I will go and carry out the behest of my lord the king. In case (however) the inhabitants of Gambûlu will not become submissive by these means, (then) if it be agreeable to my lord the king, let an envoy of my lord the king come ; let us assemble all Babylonia ; and let us go with him, win back the country, and give it to my lord the king.

I send (my advice) to my lord the king, let my lord the king do as he pleases. Preserve this letter.

ACCENTED TRANSLITERATION.

[1]*Ana šar mâtâti, belii̯a,* [2]*ardúka Nabû-ušabšî !*

[3]*Uruk u E-anna* [4]*ana šar mâtâti, belii̯a, likrubû !*

[5]*Ûmussu Ištar Uruk* [6]*u Nanâ ana balâṭ napšâte* [7]*ša šarri belii̯a uçallû !*

Ša šarru belú'a [8]*išpura, umma :* "*Xi'lânu* [9]*tušaçbat-ma, ana muxxi âl Gambûlu* [10]*tašápar.*" *Ilâni ša šarri belii̯a* [11]*lû îdû kî ultu muxxi* [12]*ša Bel-iqîša ina qât šarri belii̯a* [13]*ikkiru, mât Elamti ildudá-ma,* [14]*bît abii̯a ixpû, u ina pâni* [15]*dâku ša axii̯a illiku,* [16]*ûmussu Šamaš lâ u* . . . . . [lines 17–20 are broken away] . . . . . (Rev.) [21]*Ennâ! ša šarru belú'a iš[puráni]* [22]*attallak u našpartu* [23]*ša šarri belii̯a ušal[lam].* [24]*Immatêma libbû agâ* [25]*âšib ina âl Gambûlu* [26]*ul ibalû, kî pâni* [27]*šarri belii̯a maxru, apil šipri* [28]*ša šarri belii̯a lilliká-ma* [29]*mât Akkadî gabbi nipxur-ma,* [30]*ittišu nillik-ma, mâti* [31]*nuterá-ma ana šarri belii̯a* [32]*niddin.*

Ana šarri belii̯a [33]*altapra, šarru belû'a,* [34]*kî ša ilá'u* [35]*lîpuš. Egirtu annîtu uçri.*

5.

K 79.

The following letter, also from Nabû-ušabšî, is published in *The Cuneiform Inscriptions of Western Asia*, vol. iv., pl. 46, no. 3 (2d ed.), and is translated by Pinches in *Transactions of the Society of Biblical Archaeology*, vi. pp. 239 ff. It contains an account of the practices of a certain Pir'i-Bel and his father Bel-eṭêr, who seem to have been Chaldean conspirators, engaged in fomenting strife between Elam and Assyria. A Bel-eṭêr, son of Nabû-šum-erêš, was carried captive to Nineveh with Dunânu, prince of Gambûlu, and he and his brother Nabû-nâ'id were there forced to desecrate the bones of their father, who had been largely instrumental in inducing Urtaku to commence hostilities against Babylonia (*K. B.*, ii. p. 258, ll. 84–91). If this was the Bel-eṭêr mentioned by Nabû-ušabšî, the source of his enmity to Assyria may be readily understood, and, in this case, the letter must be referred to a later date than the preceding one (K 528).

On the other hand, it is quite possible that the similarity of names is merely a coincidence, and the events here narrated may have preceded the revolt of Bel-iqîša and the invasion of Urtaku. Kudurru, who is mentioned below, was doubtless the governor of Erech referred to above in connection with Bel-ibnî. The letter may be rendered as follows :

TRANSLATION.

To the king of the world, my lord, thy servant Nabû-ušabšî !

May Erech and E-anna be gracious to the king of the world, my lord ! I pray daily to Ištar of Erech and to Nanâ for the life of my lord the king.

Pir'i-Bel, son of Bel-eṭêr, with his father, having gone forth to Elam some ten years ago, came from Elam to Babylonia with his father. Having come (hither), they practiced in Erech all that was evil towards Assyria. Having subsequently retired to Elam, his father, Bel-eṭêr, died in Elam, and he in the month of Marcheshvan, having brought letters to me and to . . . . . . the governor, we sent(?) the letters which he brought by Dâru-šarru to (?) . . . . . .[1] . . . . . . If he tell the king, my lord, "I am come from Elam," let not the king, my lord, believe him. From the month of Marcheshvan, when we sent to my lord the king the letters he brought, until the present time he has not been to Elam. Should the king, my lord, desire confirmation of these words, Idû'a, the servant of Kudurru, who (brought ?) to Erech these reports about him(?) . . . . . .[2] let these men tell my lord the king how these treasonable letters were written, and if my lord the king does not understand about these letters which we sent in Marcheshvan to my lord the king by Dâru-šarru, let my lord the king question Dâru-šarru the satellite. I send to my lord in order that he may be informed.

ACCENTED TRANSLITERATION.

[1]*Ana šar mâtâte, beliịa,* [2]*ardûka Nabû-ušabšî !*

[3]*Uruk u E-anna ana šar mâtâte* [4]*beliịa likrubû !*

Ûmussu [5]*Ištar, Uruk, u Nanâ* [6]*ana balâṭ napšâte ša šarri beliịá-ma* [7]*uçallî !*

Pir'i-Bel, apilšu ša Bel-eṭêr, [8]*šanâte agâ* x *ultu bîd ana* [9]*mât Elamti šû u abišu ûçû,* [10]*ultu mât Elamti ana mât Akkadî* [11]*illikûni, šû u abišu.* [12]*Kî illikûni, mimma ša ana* [13]*muxxi mât Aššur bîšu ina Uruk* [14]*êtepšû. Arkâniš, ana mât Elamti* [15]*kî ixxisû, Bel-eṭêr abušu* [16]*ina mât Elamti mîtu,* [17]*u šû ina libbi*

---

[1] The text is here completely broken away. The translation is resumed at line 10 of the reverse.

[2] The text is here very uncertain.

Araxšâmna šipireti [18]*ana pâni̯a u ana pâni . . . . . .* [19]*paxâti kî iššâ, ši[pire]ti* [20]*[ša iš]šâ' ina qât Dâru-[šarru] . . . . . .* [From obverse l. 20 to reverse l. 7, the text is destroyed]. . . . . . (Rev.) *. . . . . .* [7]*enna išten qallu ša . . . . . .* [8]*ittišu ana Uruk ilta . . . . . .* [9]*Mandêma ana šarri beli̯a iqâbî,* [10]*umma: "Ultu mât Elamti attalka,"* [11]*šarru belû'a la iqâpšu. Ultu bîd ina Araxšâmna* [12]*šipirêti iššâ-ma ana šarri beli̯a* [13]*nušebila adî ša enna ana mât Elamti* [14]*ul ixxis. Kî šarru belû'a xarâçu* [15]*ša dibbe agâ çibû, ana Idû'a* [16]*qallu ša Kudurra ša ana Uruk* [17]*dibbešu* (?) *agâ idatsu* . . . . . .* [19]*šunûti-ma šipirêti* [20]*agâ ša šârâte kî ša šaṭrâ* [21]*ana šarri beli̯a liqbû, u kî* [22]*ša šipirêti agâ, ša ina libbi Araxšâmna* [23]*ina qât Dâru-šarru ana šarri beli̯a* [24]*nušebila, šarru belû'a lâ xassu,* [25]*Dâru-šarru mutîr-pûtu šarru* [26]*belû'a liš'al. Ana šarri beli̯a* [27]*altapra, šarru belû'a lû îdî.*

Another letter from Nabû-ušabšî to the king (K 514) is published, with transliteration, translation, commentary, and additional notes, by Pinches, in S. A. Smith's *Keilschrifttexte Asurbanipals*, iii. pp. 59–62, 105, 106; compare also Bezold's *Cat. of the K Collection*, p. 120. The mutilation of lines 14–17 somewhat obscures the sense; but the latter refers chiefly to horses—some of which appear to have been presented to the goddess Ištar of Erech by the King of Elam—purchased for the king of Assyria by Nabû-ušabšî, who promises to forward vouchers for the expense incurred.

6.

K 824.

K 824 is published with transliteration, translation, and commentary in S. A. Smith's *Keilschrifttexte Asurbanipals*, ii. pp. 63–67. Sin-tabnî-uçur ("Sin protect my offspring"), to whom it is addressed, was the son of Ningal-iddina ("Ningal has given"), and was governor of Ur, in Southern Babylonia, during the rebellion of Šamaš-šum-ukîn, king of Babylon and brother of Sardanapallus. Kudurru, governor of Erech, writes to King Sardanapallus that he has received a message from Sin-tabnî-uçur to the effect that an emissary of Šamaš-šum-ukîn, engaged in disseminating revolution through the country, has approached him with the view of engaging him in the treasonable design; that a portion of the district under his authority has already revolted; and that unless reinforcements be promptly sent he has the gravest fears for the result. Kudurru, in answer to this urgent appeal,

---

* The text of line 18, and of the opening words of line 19, is very uncertain. See Part II.

has sent a force to his assistance (K 5457; Winckler, *Sammlung von Keilschrifttexten*, ii. p. 55, ll. 6 ff.). According to Geo. Smith (*Hist. of Assurbanipal*, p. 201), followed by Tiele (*Bab.-Assyr. Gesch.*, pp. 377, 381), Sin-tabnî-uçur, unable to hold out until the arrival of these reinforcements, was constrained against his will to join the rebels.

The evidence that he did so, however, is by no means conclusive. His name is mentioned, it is true, in connection with that of Šamaš-šum-ukîn in two extracts from so-called omen-tablets published in Geo. Smith's work (pp. 184, 185); but the context is in both instances obscure, owing to mutilation of the text, and his participation in the rebellion, of which there is no other evidence, is merely an inference derived from the juxtaposition of the two names. Both these tablets would seem, however, to belong to the class of texts so ably illustrated in Knudtzon's *Gebete an den Sonnengott*, containing requests for information addressed to the oracles of the gods. It was by no means unusual to consult the oracle in this way with reference to an official, especially when recently appointed, or when about to be entrusted with some important commission; and several instances are given in Knudtzon's work (cf. e. g. nos. 67, 112, 114, 115). Now the first of the above mentioned tablets (K 4696), dated in the month of Ab, 651 B. C., contains the words, "Sin-tabnî-uçur, son of Ningal-iddina, who has been appointed governor of Ur" (literally, "over Ur"), which would seem to indicate that his appointment was recent; while in the second (K 28), dated in the preceding month of Tammuz, his name occurs without mention of Ur. It seems likely, therefore, that he was appointed governor of Ur in the month of Ab, 651, and that both tablets contain inquiries, addressed to the oracle, with reference to his probable conduct towards Šamaš-šum-ukîn, who was at that time in open rebellion. Unfortunately, both texts are badly mutilated, and only portions of them are published; but, in the absence of other evidence, the participation of Sin-tabnî-uçur in the great revolt can hardly be regarded as an established fact.

The letter here translated (K 824) was probably written some time before these events. Ummanigaš, mentioned in it as one of the calumniators of Sin-tabnî-uçur, was one of the three sons of Urtaku who took refuge at the Assyrian court when their father was dethroned and murdered by his brother Teumman. With the aid of Assyrian troops furnished by Sardanapallus, he defeated Teumman, who was slain in the battle, and Ummanigaš thus became king of Elam; but he was subsequently so ungrateful as to ally himself with Šamaš-šum-ukîn. In 651 or 650 B. C., he was, in his turn, deposed and slain by his brother Tammaritu, who after a brief reign was, in the year 650 B. C., deposed by Indabigaš, and with difficulty made his escape to Babylonia, whence, as already narrated, he was sent on to Assyria by Bel-ibnî, governor of the Gulf District. It was probably while residing at the Assyrian court, or at least prior to his alliance with the rebellious brother of Sardanapallus, that he endeavored to cast suspicion on the loyalty of Sin-tabnî-uçur. His accusations were not listened to by the king, who expresses the highest regard for, and the utmost confidence in, the integrity of his servant. The text may be translated as follows:

TRANSLATION.

Message of the King to Sin-tabnî-uçur. It is well with me; may thy heart be of good cheer!

With reference to thy message about Sin-šarra-uçur, how could he speak evil words of thee, and I listen to them? Since Šamaš perverted his understanding,[1] and Ummanigaš slandered thee before me, they have sought thy death, but Ašur my god withholds me (from that), and not willingly could I have put to death my servant and the support of my father's house. No!—for thou wouldst (be willing to) perish along with thy lord's house—(never) could I consent to that. He and Ummanigaš have plotted thy destruction, but because I know thy loyalty I have conferred even greater favor (than before) upon thee; is it not so? These two years thou hast not brought foe and need upon thy lord's house.[2] What could they say against a servant who loves his lord's house, that I could believe? And with regard to the service which thou and thy brother Assyrians have rendered, about which thou sendest (word), all that (?) ye have done, the guard for me which ye have kept[3] ...... and this ..... which is most honorable in my sight, and a favor which I shall require to thee till (the times of our) children's children.

ACCENTED TRANSLITERATION.

[1] *Amât šarri ana Sin-tabnî-uçur!*

[2] *Šulmu i̯âši, libbaka* [3] *lû ṭâbka!*

[4] *Ina muxxi Sin-šarra-uçur* [5] *ša tašpur, minâma dibbeka* [6] *bîšûtu iqabâ-ma* [7] *u anâku ašemîš?*

[8] *Ištu Šamaš libbašu issuxa* [9] *u Ummanigaš qarçeka* [10] *ina pâni̯a ekulu, ana* [11] *dâki iddinûka.* [12] *U Ašur ilani̯â* [13] *urâqani-ma* [14] *šuxdû-ma arda'a* [15] *u išdu ša bît abi̯a* [16] *lâ adûku.* [17] *Ul—ina libbi ša itti* [18] *bît belika* [19] *qatâta* (Rev.) [20] *lâmur agâ. Šû u* [21] *Ummanigaš ana muxxi* [22] *dâkiku ilmû,* [23] *u, ina libbi ša kenûtka* [24] *îdû, uttîr remu* [25] *aškunáka—i̯ânû?*

---

[1] The meaning is that he must be out of his senses to make such accusations.

[2] Although in that time he had ample opportunity to do so.

[3] Text mutilated.

[26]*Šanîta agâ šanâte* [27]*nakru u bubûti* [28]*ina muxxi bît belika* [29]*ul tašdud. Minû* [30]*iqabûnî-ma ina muxxi* [31]*ardi ša bît belišu irâmu* [32]*u anâku aqîpu'?*

[33]*U ina muxxi dulla ša atta u* [34]*Aššurâ axeka* [35]*tepušâ', ša tašpur,* [36]*ban ša tepušâ',* [37]*maççartá'a ša taççu[râ'].* [38]AB. AN. AN. . . . . . . , (Edge) [39]*u* MU. GA *agâ, ša ina pânija banû, u ṭâbâte* [40]*ša utâráka ana libbi ša ana mâr mâre.*

7.

K 469.

This letter, published in Harper's *Letters of the K Collection*, No. 138, carries us back to an earlier period than those treated above. The writer, Ša-Ašur-dubbu, was governor of the important city and district of Tuškhan, on the easterly course of the northwestern bend of the Tigris, which had been a possession of Assyria since at least 880 B. C., and in all probability much earlier (Tiele, *Bab.-Assyr. Gesch.*, pp. 180, 181). In 707 B. C., the sixteenth year of the reign of Sargon, the conqueror of Samaria, Ša-Ašur-dubbu gave his name to the year as Eponym, a fact which marks him as a magnate of the highest order (*K. B.*, i. pp. 207, 214). In another letter (K 1067 ; Harper, No. 139), which is unfortunately so mutilated that the context cannot be made out with certainty, he mentions the city of Penzâ, the king of the Armenian district Urartu, and a certain Khutešub. The latter, for whose name the reading Bagtišub is with great probability suggested by the Rev. C. H. W. Johns (*PSBA.*, xvii. p. 234), appears in Harper's work (No. 215=K 1037) as the author of a report, also badly mutilated, with reference to the neighboring countries of Urartu, Man, and Zikirtu, against which king Sargon (reigned 722–705 B. C.) waged successful wars in 715–714 B. C.

In the letter here translated (K 469), Ša-Ašur-dubbu gives, with military terseness, an account of a treacherous attack made upon a small party of his soldiers by a certain native of Šupria, a district which apparently lay near Tuškhan, in the corner formed by the northwestern Tigris, where it turns its course eastward (cf. Knudtzon's *Gebete an den Sonnengott*, ii. p. 151).

The city of Dûr-Šarrukîn, or "Sargonsburg," mentioned in line 20 of the reverse, and for which the timber mentioned in line 17 was probably required, was founded, after a long cherished plan, by the great king whose name it commemorates, and completed in the latter years of his reign. On the 22^d^ of Tishri (September), 707, in the eponymy of Ša-Ašur-dubbu, the images of the gods were carried through its streets in solemn procession, and established in their temples, and in April of the following year the king formally took up his residence in his new capital. One year later (705), he fell by the hand of an assassin (Tiele, *Bab.-Assyr. Gesch.*, p. 248). The site of Dûr-Šarrukîn, occupied by the modern village of Khorsabad, was explored in the years 1843–1844 by the French consul at Mosul, Émile Botta, who discovered the palace of Sargon, with a wealth of sculptures and inscriptions which were conveyed to Paris, and now form part of the Louvre collection. The letter of Ša-Ašur-dubbu may be rendered as follows:

TRANSLATION.

To the king, my lord, thy servant Ša-Ašur-dubbu! A hearty greeting to the king, my lord! Greeting to the fortresses, to the country of the king my lord!

I sent two of my officers, accompanied by six men and provided with a warrant, after some deserters who were in the city of Penzâ. Two chiefs of battalion went along with them. The soldiers took down rations, of which they partook (en route). The brother of the Šuprian, having shared their meal with them, they set out and travelled along together. The Šuprian had laid an ambush beforehand, (but) the two officers, with the six soldiers, got out (of it, and) rescued both the chiefs of battalion. I sent word to them, "Establish (there) a military post." I shall make an investigation, (and) if they are in my country I shall lay hands on the rascals. I went and brought up troops into the fortress. Let the king, my lord, send orders that the Taziru and the Itû of my lord the king, who have appointed their deputies here, may come (themselves) and stand guard with me, until they get this timber away. The king, my lord, shall decide. My men are doing duty in Dûr-Šarrukîn, (but) the cavalry are here with me.

ACCENTED TRANSLITERATION.

[1] *Ana šarri, belii̯a,* [2] *ardúka Ša-Ašur-dubbu!*

[3] *Lû šulmu ana šarri,* [4] *belii̯a, adanniš!*

[5] *Šulmu ana âl bîrât,* [6] *ana mâti ša šarri belii̯a!*

[7] II *rešei̯a,* VI *çâbe* [8] *issišunu, kunukku ina qâtišunu,* [9] *ina muxxi xalqûte, ša ina âl Penzâ* [10] *assaparšunu.* II *rabe-qiçir* [11] *issišunu ittallakû.* [12] *Çâbe usseridûni* [13] *akâle, ina libbi etaklû.* [14] *Axušu ša Šupri'â* [15] *issišunu ina libbi* [16] *etakla. Qa....ni axiš* [17] *ittúçûni,* [18] *ittalkûni.* [19] *Šupri'â* [20] *šubtu ina pânâtu* [21] *ussešibu.* (Rev.) [1] II *rešei̯a* [2] *itti* VI *çâbe ittaçû,* [3] *rabe-qiçirii̯a* [4] *kilale ussezibû.* [5] *Assaparášunu 'šubat çâbe* [6] *rammî'. Mâ, aš'al;* [7] *šumma ina mâtii̯a šunu, addan* [8] *anâku qâtâ'a ina kibsâti.* [9] *Attallak, çâbe ina* [10] *bîrtišu usselî'a.* [11] *Taziru, Itu'u* [12] *ša šarri*

beliia, ša annaka[11] *uqa'ib(û?)**-*ni šaknûtišunu*, [12]*šarru belî lišpura* [13]*lillikûni, issia ana* [14]*maççarti lizzizû*, [15]*adî gušûre annûte* [16]*ušeçûni. Šarru belî* [17]*ûdâ. Câbeia* [18][*ina*] *âl Dûr-Šarrukîn* [19][*dul*]*la ippušû*, (Edge) [20]*ša bithallâti šunu ina pâniia* [21]*izzazû.*

8.

K 629.

The worship of the god Nabû seems to have been introduced into Assyria from Babylonia,—where he was from early times the special divinity of the important city of Borsippa near Babylon,—during the reign of Rammân-nirârî III. (812–783 B. C.), before which time the god would seem to have played no prominent part in the Assyrian pantheon. The annotated Eponym Canon records that in the year 787 the god Nabû made solemn entry into his "new temple" (*K. B.*, i. p. 210), and this temple, situated in the city of Calah, where its ruins have been explored, bore, like its famous Babylonian prototype, the name of Ezida, "the true house." Upon two statues of Nabû found by W. K. Loftus in the temple at Calah, is an inscription (identical in both cases) stating that these statues were prepared by Bel-tarçi-ilu-ma, governor of Calah and the adjoining district, as a votive offering "for the life of Rammân-nirârî, king of Assyria, his lord, and Sammu-râmat, the lady of the palace, his lady," as also for his own welfare and that of his family (*K. B.*, i. p. 192).

Sammu-râmat, whose name recalls that of the mythical Semiramis,[1] was either the wife or mother of the king; and Tiele argues with great plausibility that this lady was a Babylonian princess, and that the introduction of the cult of Nabû into Assyria was owing to her influence (Tiele, *Bab-Assyr. Gesch.*, pp. 207, 212). Once established, the worship of the god took firm root, and continued to flourish down to the last days of the empire.

Nabû-šum-iddina ("Nabû has given a name"), who, in the letter here presented describing a religious ceremony and solemn procession in honor of the god, styles himself the prefect of the temple of Nabû, appears to have lived in the reign of Esarhaddon; and the prince to whom the letter is addressed was proba-

---

* Harper's text reads here *u-ka-ip-ni* (i. e. *uqâ'ip*, II. 1. of *qâpu*, st. קיף), but the enclitic *ni* cannot be joined to the verb without a union vowel (cf. Del., *Assyr. Gram.*, § 79, *β*), and in any case we should expect the *modus relativus* after the preceding *ša*. The insertion of *u* improves both the sense and the construction. For *itû* as an official title, see Delitzsch, *Handw.*, p. 157a, and *PSBA.*, May 1889, pl. iv. col. i. 18; col. ii. 11.

[1] Cf. *Beitr. zur Assyr.*, i. p. 323 below.

bly Sardanapallus, and was evidently the heir to the throne, since a wish is expressed for the long duration of his future reign. A letter to the king from the same writer, or from a person of the same name (K 1017 ; Harper, No. 66), is too badly mutilated to yield any connected sense, but mentions (rev. ll. 1, 2) the crown prince (*mâr šarri rabû ša bît-ridûte*), and the name of Sardanapallus, of which traces are preserved, is evidently to be restored before the title.

Fourteen letters (Nos. 60–73) are published in Harper's work under the name of Nabû-šum-iddina. Of Nos. 72 (K 1272) and 73 (K 5509) merely the opening words remain ; and the context of Nos. 67 (K 1050) and 70 (K 1070) is rendered unintelligible by the mutilation of the tablet. No. 66 has just been referred to, and all the rest are reports of the arrival of horses.[1] Whether the priest of Nabû and the writer about horses were identical is open to doubt. The formula of greeting is certainly the same in the letters of both persons, but it is not a very characteristic one. The invocation to Nabû and Marduk is common to many writers; precisely the same formula is found, for example, in the letter of Nabû-nâçir ("Nabû protects") to the king (Harper, No. 178=K 482).

The ceremonies attending the consecration of the couch of a god, referred to in the letter before us, are minutely described in a liturgical text (K 164; *Beitr. zur Assyr.*, ii. p. 635). After the appropriate offerings are presented, the officiating priestess purifies the feet of the divine image with a sprig of reed and a vessel of oil, approaches (?) the bed three times, kisses the feet of the image, and retires and sits down. She then burns cedar wood dipped in wine, places before the image the heart of a sheep wrapped in a cloth, and offers libations. Aromatic woods are consecrated and burnt, further libations and offerings are made, tables are spread for various divinities, and the ceremony concludes with a prayer for the king. This recalls Herodotus' description (i. 181) of the temple of Bel-Merodach at Babylon, where it is stated that the chamber containing the couch of the god, beside which stood a golden table, was at night occupied only by a woman supposed to be chosen by the god himself from all the women of the country. It would appear from the text before us that stables were attached to the temples for the accommodation of horses used on ceremonial occasions, when a specially appointed charioteer officiated. The jar-bearers mentioned probably carried holy water for lustral purposes and wine for libations.

The letter of Nabû-šum-iddina (K 629=Harper, No. 65) may be thus translated :

---

[1] For translations of most of these, and of other letters upon the same subject, see Delitzsch in *Beitr. zur Assyr.*, i. pp. 202-212 ; ii. pp. 44-55.

TRANSLATION.

To the prince, my lord, thy servant Nabû-šum-iddina!

A hearty, hearty greeting to the prince, my lord! May Nabû and Marduk bless the prince, my lord!

On the third day of the month of Iyyar the city of Calah will consecrate the couch of Nabû, (and) the god will enter the bed-chamber. On the fourth (will take place) the return of Nabû. The prince my lord shall decide. I am the prefect of the house of Nabû thy god, (so) I (of course) shall go.

At Calah the god will come forth from the palace enclosure (?), (and) from the palace enclosure (?) will go to the grove. A sacrifice will be offered. The charioteer of the gods, coming from the stable of the gods, will take the god forth, bring him back, and convey him within. This is the route of the procession.

Of the jar-bearers, whoever has a sacrifice (to offer) will offer it. Whoever offers up one *qa*[1] of his food, may enter the house of Nabû. May they[2] perfectly execute the ordinances of the gods, to the life and health of the prince, my lord. What (commands) has the prince, my lord, to send me? May Bel and Nabû, who granted help in the month of Shebat, guard the life of the prince, my lord. May they make thy sovereignty extend to the end of time.

ACCENTED TRANSLITERATION.

[1]*Ana mâr šarri beli̯a,* [2]*ardúka Nabû-šum-iddina!*

[3]*Lû šulmu ana mâr šarri beli̯a* [4]*adanniš adanniš!*

[5]*Nabû, Marduk ana mâr šarri* [6]*beli̯a likrubû!*

[7]*Ûmu šâlšu ša arax Âri âl Kalxi* [8]*eršu ša Nabû takárar.* [9]*Nabû ina bît erši errab.* [10]*Ûmu rebû târšu ša Nabû.* [11]*Mâr šarri belî ûdâ.* [12am]*xazânu ša bît Nabû* [13]*iluka anâku,* [14]*lallik. Ina âl Kalxi* [15]*ilu ina libbi adri ekalli* [16]*uçâ, ša libbi adri ekalli* [17]*ana kirî illaka.* [18]*Niqû* (Edge) [19]*innépaš.* [20][*Ina*] *urû ša ilâni* [21]*mukîl-asâte* (Rev.) [1]*ša ilâní-ma illak,* [2]*ilu ušeçâ* [3]*u ussaxxar* [4]*ušerab. Šû* [5]*etêqa illaka.* [6]*Nâš-šappâte, ša niqûšu* [7]*ibášúni, ippaš.* [8]*Ša* 1 QA *aklišu ušelâ,* [9]*ina bît Nabû errab.* [10]*Parçe ša ilâni šunu,* [11]*ana bulluṭ napšâte* [12]*ša mâr šarri beli̯a,* [13]*lušallimû lipušû.* [14]*Mînu ša mâr šarri* [15]*belî išáparáni?* [16]*Bel, Nabû, ša ina arax Šabâṭi* [17]*xamaṭṭa iškunûni,* [18]*napšâte ša mâr šarri* (Edge) [19]*beli̯a liççurû,* [20]*šarrûtka* [21]*ana çât ûme lušâlikû.*

---

[1] A measure; cf. p. 141, l. 56.

[2] Those officiating at the ceremony.

9.

K 547.

The general tone of this letter, and the reference to the gods Bel and Nabû contained in it, would seem to favor the identification of the writer with the priest of Nabû who in the text last treated invokes the same deities in behalf of the prince. The title of the official to whom it is addressed is mutilated, and is here restored in accordance with the traces given in Harper's copy of the text, which is published in his *Letters of the K Collection* (No. 62). It is a courteous expression of the good wishes of the writer in connection, apparently, with some matter the nature of which is not stated, but was of course well known to the recipient.

TRANSLATION.

To the Secretary of State, my lord, thy servant Nabû-šum-iddina! Greeting to my lord!

May Nabû and Marduk, Ištar of Nineveh, Ištar of Arbela, bless my lord! May they keep thee whole! May thy heart ever be of good cheer! May Bel and Nabû establish prosperity in the homes of the people of Nineveh and prosperity with thee also.

ACCENTED TRANSLITERATION.

[1]*Ana* [*dupšar*] *mâti* [2]*beliịa, ardûka* [3]*Nabû-šum-iddina!*

[4]*Lû šulmu ana beliịa!*

[5]*Nabû u Marduk,* [6]*Ištar ša Ninua,* [7]*Ištar ša Arba'il* [8]*ana beliịa* [9]*likrubû!* [10]*Lušallimûka!*

(Rev.) [1]*Libbaka* [2]*ka'âmâni* [3]*lû ṭâba!* [4]*Šulmu ina bîti* [5]*ana nîšê* [6]*ša ina Ninua,* [7]*u šulmu* [8]*issika* [9]*Bel u Nabû* [10]*lipqidû!*

10.

K 589.

Išdî-Nabû ("Nabû is my foundation"), an Assyrian official who probably flourished in the reign of Esarhaddon (681–668 B. C.), is the writer of four letters published in Harper's collection (Nos. 186–189). In one of them (K 1048; Harper, No. 189), of which there remains only the formula of greeting and the name of one Ašur-šezibâni ("Ašur deliver me"), a governor, about whom some communication apparently followed, he styles himself, "the secretary of the new house." Another (K 113; Harper, No. 186)[1] contains a salutation "to the guards of the

---

[1] Published with transliteration, translation, and commentary by S. A. Smith, *Keilschrifttexte Asurbanipals*, iii. pp. 18–21 (with additional notes by Pinches, pp. 91–93); also by Delitzsch, *Beiträge zur Assyr.*, ii. pp. 24–30.

king, my lord," and refers chiefly to the endeavor of a certain Nâdin-šum-ilu ("the god gives a name") to recruit for the same corps fifty men, formerly under the command of his father, who met his death "in the land of the enemy." The letter, written at Nineveh, is addressed to the king, who would seem to have been at the time in the neighborhood of Sippara. The second letter (K 589; Harper, No. 187), addressed to the prince (literally "the son of the king"), who may have been Sardanapallus, contains a courtly greeting, and conveys the assurance of the good will of the god Nabû, whose oracle he had doubtless consulted. It may be thus rendered :

TRANSLATION.

To the prince, my lord, thy servant Išdî-Nabû! A hearty greeting to the prince, my lord! May Bel, Nabû, Belit the divine queen of Kidimuri, and Ištar of Arbela grant health of mind and body, life, and happiness to the prince, my lord!

I convey the gracious messages of Nabû. Greeting to all the guard! May the heart of the prince, my lord, be of good cheer.

ACCENTED TRANSLITERATION.

[1]*Ana mâr šarri beliia,* [2]*ardúka Išdî-Nabû !*

[3]*Lû šulmu ana mâr šarri* [4]*beliia adanniš !*

[5]*Bel, Nabû,* [6]*Belit iltu belit Kidimuri,* [7]*Ištar ša Arba'il* [8]*ṭûb libbi,* [9]*ṭûb šîre,* [10]*lale balâṭi* [11]*ana mâr šarri beliia* [12]*liddinû !*

(Rev.) [1]*Rixâte* [2]*ša Nabû* [3]*ana mâr šarri beliia* [4]*ussebila.* [5]*Šulmu ana maççarâte* [6]*gabbu! Libbu* [7]*ša mâr šarri beliia* [8]*lû ṭâbšu !*

11.

K 551.

The importance attributed to omens, and the great attention paid to their interpretation by the Assyro-Babylonians, is attested by the very large number of tablets dealing with the subject found in the ruined temples and palaces of the ancient Mesopotamian empires.[1] These texts, which would seem to have accumulated from a very remote period, contain explanations of omens derived from phenomena of every description, terrestrial as well as celestial, and were consulted as the standard authorities, whenever, as often happened, such information was desired.

The astrologer Nabû'a doubtless had in mind a passage from one of these tablets when he wrote the letter here translated. At precisely what period this votary of astral science lived and

---

[1] Cf. Alfred Boissier, *Documents assyriens relatifs aux présages*, Paris, 1894 ff.

practiced his art, it is impossible to say with certainty; but it was in all probability under one of the Sargonide kings. In two observatory reports published in *The Cuneiform Inscriptions of Western Asia*, vol. iii. p. 51, he signs his name, "Nabû'a of the City of Aššur," the ancient capital of Assyria. In a similar communication (Harper, No. 141=K 481), he reports that an observation had been made, and that the sun and moon had been visible in the heavens at the same time.

The omen to be derived from the occurrence mentioned below was doubtless an unfavorable one, since otherwise the fox would hardly have been killed. That the fox, however, was not invariably regarded as a harbinger of evil may be gathered from two passages from an omen-text relating to the building of a house, published in Pinches' *Texts in the Babylonian Wedge-Writing*, p. 12. The first (obv. col. i, ll. 30–33) may be thus rendered: "When the foundations are laid, if green locusts are seen, the foundations will go to ruin and the house will not be constructed. If black locusts are seen, the owner of the house will die an untimely death. If either a fox or locusts (?) are seen, the house will go to ruin. If dogs and swine fight, the house will have a claimant (at law)." In the second passage, however, the appearance of the fox was regarded as a good omen, since we read (*ibid.* obv. col. 2, ll. 1 ff.): "When the threshold is laid, if a fox enters the house, the house will be inhabited. If locusts (?) enter the house, the house will go to ruins. If an ox, misfortune will overtake the house. If a horse, the wife of the owner will die. If an ass, the son of the owner will die," etc. The letter of Nabû'a (K 551; Harper, No. 142) may be translated as follows:

TRANSLATION.

To the king, my lord, thy servant Nabû'a!

May Nabû and Marduk bless the king, my lord!

On the seventh day of the month Kislev a fox entered the city, and fell into a well in the grove of the god Ašur. They got him out, and killed him.

ACCENTED TRANSLITERATION.

[1]*Ana šarri belija* [2]*ardûka Nabû'a!*

[3]*Nabû Marduk* [4]*ana šarri belija* [5]*likrubû!*

[6]*Ûmu sebû ša arax Kisilimi* [7]*šelibu ina libbi âli* [8]*etarba,* [9]*ina kirî ša Ašur* (Rev.) [1]*ina bûri ittuqut.* [2]*Usselûni* [3]*idûkû.*

12.

K 565.

Balasi, the author of six letters published in Harper's work (Nos. 74–79), all relating to astrology, divination, and kindred matters, and also of a number of astrological reports (cf., e. g.

III R 51, no. iv; 54, no. 10; 58, no. 12), was an Assyrian priestly astrologer who lived in the reign of Esarhaddon (681–668 B. C.). He was therefore a contemporary of Arad-Ea, Arad-Nanâ, and Nabû-šum-iddina, examples of whose correspondence are given in this paper, Nos. 8, 13, 14 and 15.

The letter of Balasi and his colleague Nabû-akhe-erba which is selected for translation here is evidently in answer to a communication from the king, who desired to be informed as to the advisability of a journey contemplated for his son Ašur-mukîn-pale'a, and the most auspicious occasion for setting out upon it. The answer is favorable; the journey may be undertaken, and though the second of the month will do very well, the fourth is particularly recommended. It may be that the prince was in ill health, and that this was the occasion of the intended journey. The physician Arad-Nanâ mentions Ašur-mukîn-pale'a in terms which would indicate that he was suffering from some malady (see p. 161). This text, which is published in Harper's Letters (No. 77), may be translated as follows:

TRANSLATION.

To the king, our lord, thy servants Balasi and Nabû-akhe-erba! Greeting to the king, our lord! May Nabû and Marduk bless the king, our lord!

As for Ašur-mukîn-pale'a, about whom the king, our lord, has sent to us, may Ašur, Bel, Nabû, Sin, Šamaš, and Rammân bless him!

May our lord the king behold his welfare.

The conditions are auspicious for the journey. The second of the month is an auspicious day; the fourth, extremely auspicious.

ACCENTED TRANSLITERATION.

[1]*Ana šarri belini,* [2]*ardânika* [3]*Balasî* [4]*Nabû-axe-erba!*

[5]*Lû šulmu* [6]*ana šarri belini!*

[7]*Nabû Marduk* [8]*ana šarri belini* [9]*likrubû!*

[10]*Ina muxxi Ašur-mukîn-paleịa,* [11]*ša šarri beluni* [12]*išpuranâšini,* [13]*Ašur, Bel, Sin,* [14]*Šamaš, Rammân* [15]*likrubûšu!* (Rev.) [1]*Nimelšu* [2]*šarru belúni lîmur!*

[3]*Ṭâba* [4]*ana alâki.* [5]*Ûmu šanû ṭâba.* [6]*Ûmu rebû adanniš* [7]*ṭâba.*

13.

K 1024.

Arad-Ea ("Servant of Ea"), the writer of K 1024, was a priest and astrologer who flourished in the reign of Esarhaddon (681-668 B. C.). He is mentioned as exercising priestly functions in a letter of the astrologer, Marduk-šakin-šum ("Merodach appoints a name"); see Harper, No. 23=K 602, obv. 19; and his name occurs in another letter of the same writer, in which the prince (i. e. Sardanapallus) and his brother Šamaš-šum-ukîn are also mentioned (Harper, No. 24=K 626, obv. 5, 6, no. 20). He also appears (Harper, No. 16=K 1428) as the joint author of an address to the king in company with his colleagues Rammân-šum-uçur ("Ramman protect the name"), Ištar-šum-ereš ("Ištar has willed a name"), and Akkullânu, all of whom are known to have lived in the reign of Esarhaddon. His functions are more precisely indicated by the fact that he is the author of a letter to the king on religious ceremonies (K 1204) and of an astrological report (K 1405). He is doubtless to be identified with the priest bearing the same name who appears in a list of officials of the reign of Esarhaddon (*PSBA.*, May, 1889, pl. iv. col. 1, 29).

In Harper's *Letters*, four letters (Nos. 27–30) are published under the name of Arad-Ea, but the last of these (No. 30=K 7426) must have been written by a person of the same name of an earlier date. It is addressed (obv. 2) to King Sargon (reigned 722–705); is written in the Babylonian, while the other three are in the Assyrian character; and differs also in the formula of greeting with which it begins. Of the remaining three, one (No. 27=K 1022) is entirely lost after the initial complimentary phrases, which are practically identical in all three, and another (No. 29=K 1204) is too badly damaged to admit of translation. Of the third (No. 28=K 1024), the last line of the obverse and the first two lines of the reverse are almost entirely obliterated, but the sense, if not the exact words, of what has been lost may be easily supplied from the context. The letter conveys to the king, who was apparently afflicted with some illness, the assurance that, by the will of the gods, he will certainly recover and live for many years to come, to which desirable end the prayers of the writer shall not be wanting.

TRANSLATION.

To the king, my lord, thy servant Arad-Ea! Greeting to my lord the king! May Nabû, Marduk, Sin, Ningal, (and) Nusku bless the king, my lord!

Sin, Ningal[1] . . . . . . shall grant life, and length (of days) to the king, my lord. I pray day and night for my lord's life.

ACCENTED TRANSLITERATION.

[1]*Ana šarri belịia* [2]*ardúka Arad-Ea!*

[3]*Lû šulmu* [4]*ana šarri belịia!*

[5]*Nabû, Marduk, Sin,* [6]*Nin-gâl, Nusku* [7]*ana šarri belịia* [8]*likrubû!*

---

[1] The text is obliterated, but the names of other gods doubtless followed here.

[9]*Sin, Nin-gal* ...... [10] ...... (Rev.) [1]...... [*bulâṭ*] [2]*napišti* [*ša ûme*] [3]*rûqûti* [4]*ana šarri belija* [5]*iddanû.*

[6]*Anâku ûmi mûšu* [7]*ina muxxi napšâte* [8]*ša belija* [9]*uçallâ.*

14.

S 1064.

According to the statement of Herodotus (i. 197), the Babylonians did not employ physicians, but brought their sick to the market-place in order to receive the advice of such persons as might be able to suggest a remedy derived from their personal experience or from that of their friends. The statement is entirely erroneous. The fact that physicians existed and were held in high esteem both in Assyria and Babylonia is abundantly attested by the cuneiform inscriptions. They belonged to the priestly class, and in their practice combined magic with more rational methods.

It was the belief that sickness was due to the agency of demons or evil spirits, which invaded the body of an individual and produced all manner of diseases. A large number of charms and incantations have been found, having for their object the expulsion of the malevolent spirits and the restoration of the sufferer. Most of these charms are fantastic in the extreme, but occasionally the magical formula veils a really sensible prescription. For example, in the *Cuneiform Inscriptions of Western Asia*, vol. iv. p. 29* (4C, col. ii, rev. ll. 6–8), is a charm for the cure of a disease of the eyes, which directs the application of crushed palm-bark; and it is immediately followed (ll. 10–26) by another, in which ground bark is recommended as a remedy for the same affection. In both these cases it is evident that the virtue of the charm lies in the astringent application recommended; it is, in fact, a measure very similar to the use of tea-leaves, a well known household remedy frequently resorted to in cases of inflamed eyes.

Among the epistolary tablets are a few letters from physicians, and from these also it may be gathered that these ancient practitioners did not entirely depend upon magic arts, as may be seen from the two examples here presented. The writer, in both cases, is Arad-Nanâ ("Servant of Nanâ"), who flourished in the reign of Esarhaddon (681–668 B. C.), and was probably court physician of that monarch. Four of his letters are published in Harper's work (No. 108–111.) In one of these (K 532, obv. 8, rev. 11) he refers to Ašur-mukîn-pale'a ("Ašur establishes my reign"), a younger son of Esarhaddon and brother of Sardanapallus, and assures the king that he need be under no apprehension (obv. 11) as to the health of the prince, who seems to have been under his professional care. In another (K 576) he directs the king to anoint himself as a precaution against draughts, to drink pure water, and to wash his hands frequently in a bowl (rev. 4–10).

The letter which follows is published, with translation, transliteration, and commentary, by S. A. Smith in his *Keilschrifttexte Asurbanipals* (ii. 58–63).[1] Mr. Smith considers that the disease was hardly a natural one, but that the patient had received one, or perhaps several wounds, one of which, affecting the head, was likely to prove mortal (p. 58). The original, however, contains no mention of a wound, nor does Arad-Nanâ seem to have any apprehension as to the result. The case, in fact, would rather seem to have been one of opththalmia or, more probably, facial erysipelas,[2] which, however, was taking a favorable course—so favorable indeed that Arad-Nanâ feels compelled to attribute it to the special interposition of some god who had interested himself in the matter. The prognosis is therefore excellent, and the complete recovery of the patient may be expected in the course of seven or eight days. The invocation to the deities Adar and Gula in the formula of salutation, is usually found in letters written by physicians, these divinities being the special patrons of the healing art. The letter may be translated as follows :

TRANSLATION.

To the king, my lord, thy servant Arad-Nanâ ! A hearty greeting to my lord the king ! May the deities Adar and Gula grant health of mind and body to my lord the king !

All goes well in regard to that poor fellow whose eyes are diseased. I had applied a dressing covering his face. Yesterday, towards evening, undoing the bandage which held it (in place), I removed the dressing. There was pus upon the dressing the size of the tip of the little finger. If any of thy gods has put his hand to the matter, that (god) must surely have given express commands.[3] All is well. Let the heart of my lord the king be of good cheer ! Within seven or eight days he will be well.

ACCENTED TRANSLITERATION.

[1]*Ana šarri beli̯a* [2]*ardúka Arad-Nanâ !*
[3]*Lû šulmu adanniš adanniš* [4]*ana šarri beli̯a !*
[5]*Adar u Gula* [6]*ṭûb libbi, ṭûb šîre* [7]*ana šarri beli̯a liddinû !*
[8]*Šulmu adanniš* [9]*ana lakû* [10]*sikru xannî'u,* [11]*ša kûri înâšu.* [12]*Talîtu ina muxxi* [13]*urtakkis, ina appišu* [14]*irtumu.* [15]*Ina timâli,* (Rev.) [16]*kî bâdi,* [17]*širṭu ša ina libbi* [18]*câbitúni aptaṭar,* [19]*talîtu ša*

---

[1] Translated also by the present writer in Johns Hopkins Circulars, No. 114 (July, 1894), p. 119.

[2] Cf. Dr. M. Bartels' paper on *ṭe'u* in the *Zeitschrift für Assyriologie*, viii. p. 179. According to Dr. Bartels, *muruç qaqqadi* ("the disease of the head") or *ṭe'u* is the Assyrian name of erysipelas.

[3] I. e. to bring about so desirable a result.

ina muxxi [20]*utûli. Šarku* [21]*ina muxxi talîti* [22]*bášî ammar qaqqad* [23]*ubâni çixirti.*

[24]*Ilânika, šumma memeni* [25]*idâšu ina libbi* [26]*ummidúni—šûtuma* [27]*pîšu ittedin.*

[28]*Šulmu adanniš.* [29]*Libbu ša šarri beli̯a* [30]*lû ṭâba !* (Edge) [31]*Adû ûme* VII VIII *ibálaṭ.*

15.

K 519.

The following letter, K 519, also from Arad-Nanâ to his royal patron Esarhaddon, is published in Harper's *Letters*, No. 108. In ll. 9–14 of the obverse the context is so interrupted and obscured by mutilation of the text that it has seemed advisable to make no attempt at translation, and these lines are accordingly omitted. The reverse, which contains all that is interesting from a medical point of view, relates to a patient suffering from severe epistaxis. External compresses seem to have been applied, which are characterized as unscientific appliances, serving only to interfere with the patient's breathing, and valueless as a means of checking the hemorrhage. Plugging the nares is the proper mode of treatment, in the opinion of Arad-Nanâ, whose letter may be rendered as follows :

TRANSLATION.

To the king, my lord, thy servant, Arad-Nanâ ! Greeting most heartily to my lord the king ! May Adar and Gula grant health of mind and body to my lord the king. A hearty greeting to the son of the king . . . . . .[1]

With regard to the patient who has a bleeding from his nose, the Rab-MUGI[2] reports : " Yesterday, towards evening, there was much hemorrhage." Those dressings are not scientifically applied. They are placed upon the alæ of the nose, oppress the breathing, and come off when there is hemorrhage. Let them be placed within the nostrils, and then the air will be kept away and the hemorrhage restrained. If it is agreeable to my lord, the king, I will go to-morrow and give instructions ; (meantime) let me hear how he does.

ACCENTED TRANSLITERATION.

[1]*Ana šarri beli̯a* [2]*ardúka Arad-Nanâ !*
[3]*Lû šulmu adanniš adanniš* [4]*ana šarri beli̯a !*
Adar [5]*u Gula ṭûb libbi,* [6]*ṭûb šîrê ana šarri beli̯a* [7]*liddinû !*
Šulmu adanniš [8]*ana mâr šarri !*

---

[1] Obverse ll. 9–14 are here omitted.
[2] An official title.

Dullu [9]*ša ana . . . . . . nipušûni* [10]*niddinuni parap kaspu. Ûmu ša* [11]*ittallak ixteridi* [12]*uktîl idâte* [13]*ittušib akî* [14]*umtal . . . . . .* (Rev.) [1]*Ina muxxi marçi* [2]*ša dâme ša appišu* [3]*illakúni, rab-mugi* [4]*iqtebîia, mâ:* [5]*"ina timâli, kî bâdi,* [6]*dâmu ma'adu* [7]*ittalkû,"— lippe* [8]*ammûte ina lâ mûdânûte* [9]*ibáši'u. Ina muxxi* [10]*naxnaxete ša appi* [11]*ummudû, naxnuxûtu* [12]*uṭâ'ubû, ištu pâni* [13]*dâme úçûni.* [14]*Pî naxîre* [15]*liškunú, šâru* [16]*ikkasir,* [17]*dâme ikkali'u.* (Edge) [18]*Šumma pân šarri maxir, ana šeri* [19]*. . . . . . ina libbi lušaxkim. Umâ šulmu lušme.*

16.

K 504.

According to the Book of Daniel (Chap. 2), Nebuchadnezzar placed the Babylonian sages in a most embarrassing predicament by requiring them to describe to him a dream which he had forgotten, alleging that their boasted science, if a reality, ought to be equal to the task, not only of furnishing an explanation in cases where the facts were known, but also of discovering the facts themselves without the aid of previous information. It is hardly likely that the two Assyrian physicians mentioned in the following letter were confronted with so difficult a problem as their Babylonian confreres of a later date, although in withholding from them all previous information in regard to the matter about which they were to be consulted, the king may have wished to apply a somewhat similar test to their science, and to secure from them a perfectly independent and unbiased opinion.

Ištar-dûrî ("Ištar is my wall"), in whose communication to the king they are mentioned, appears in Harper's work as the author of eight letters. All of them, except the one here translated, are either badly mutilated or merely fragmentary, but from what remains the personality of the writer can be established with very little doubt. In one (Harper, No. 159=K 1025) he mentions (ll. 4–5) "the cavalry of Nibe." From the inscriptions of Sargon we learn that, on the death of Daltâ, king of Ellip, a country lying immediately north of Elam, his two sons, Nibe and Išpabarra, went to war with one another about the succession to the throne. The former allied himself with the king of Elam, the latter appealed for aid to Sargon. Accordingly, in the year 708 B. C., an Assyrian army invaded Ellip, defeated Nibe and his Elamite allies, and placed Išpabarra on the throne (Sargon, *Annals*, 402–411; *Khorsabad*, 117–121). It was doubtless this Nibe who is mentioned by Ištar-dûrî.

In another letter (Harper, No. 158=K 530), the name of Merodach-baladan occurs (obv. 22); and though the context is completely obliterated, it is probable at least that this was the Chaldean prince who made himself king of Babylon in 721 B. C., but was expelled by Sargon in 710, and took refuge in Elam—the same Merodach-baladan whose message to king Hezekiah is related in Isaiah xxxix. Nabû-zer-ibnî ("Nabû has created offspring"), chief of Ru'a, is mentioned in the same letter (obv. 4), and the people of Ru'a were one of the Aramean tribes who surrendered to Sargon in 712 B. C., and were joined to the new province of Gambûlu (*Annals*, 264–271; Winckler, *Keilschrifttexte Sargons*, i. p. xxxiv). In the letter here translated, mention is made of Šamaš-bel-uçur ("Šamaš protect my lord"), who sends a communication from Der; and a Šamaš-bel-uçur, who may well have been the same person, was eponym in the year 710 B. C. (*K. B.*, i. p. 205).[1]

All these circumstances point to the reign of Sargon (722–705 B. C.) as the period in which Ištar-dûrî flourished, and, as an Ištar-dûrî was eponym in the year 714 (*K. B.*, i. p. 205), we shall probably not be far wrong if we conclude that the writer of the letters and the eponym were one and the same person. This identification was also proposed by the late Geo. Smith, who states in his *Assyrian Eponym Canon* (p. 85), under the year 714 B. C.: "Ištar-duri, the eponym of this year, sent the two Tablets K 1068 and 504."

The former (K 1068), as yet unpublished, is, according to Bezold's Catalogue, a letter to the king about astrological forecasts; the latter (K 504) is the letter which forms the subject of this number. It is published in Harper's *Letters*, No. 157, and also, with transliteration, translation, and commentary, by S. A. Smith in the *Proceedings of the Society of Biblical Archæology*, x. pp. 168 ff. The version here given is offered as a substitute for that of Mr. Smith.

The city of Der, for whose temples copies of inscriptions are requested, was a seat of the worship of the god Anu, and was situated towards the Babylonian and Elamite frontier, in the district lying between the lower course of the Tigris and the Median mountains (Mürdter-Delitzsch, *Gesch. Babyl.-Assyr.*, p. 175). It must have contained a sanctuary of some celebrity, since the

---

[1] The following texts bearing upon Šamaš-bel-uçur and the city of Der are registered in Bezold's *Catalogue of the K Collection*:—K 5193. A letter to the king; mentions the king of Elam, and the cities Der, Mandiri'a, and Khalçu.—K 6122. A letter to the king; mentions the king of Elam, the city of Der, etc.—K 7297. A letter to the king; mentions Šamaš-bel-uçur.—K 7299. A letter to the king from Šamaš-bel-uçur; reports the entry of the king of Elam into the Elamite city of Bit-Bunaki, etc.; mentions the cities of Der and Khalçu.—K 7325. A letter to the king; mentions Šamaš-bel-uçur, Marduk-sallima, and the city of Khalçu—K 7424. A letter to the king from Šamaš-bel-uçur; mentions the king of Elam and the cities of Der and Khalçu.—K 8535. A letter to the king from Šamaš-bel-uçur; mentions Balasu.

A letter to the king from Šamaš-bel-uçur, published by Harper in *Zeitschrift für Assyr.*, viii. p. 343, mentions neither Ištar-dûrî nor the city of Der.

annotated Eponym List records that in the years 815 and 785 B. C. "the great god went to Der," which means that his image was carried thither in solemn procession. It is possible that, as was conjectured by the late Geo. Smith, Der is to be identified with the city of Dûr-ili, often mentioned in the inscriptions. (See *Beitr. zur Assyr.*, iii. p. 238, 42 ; 282, 42). For references to the city in connection with Elam, see the note on Šamaš-bel-uçur above. It is to be hoped that the site of this city may yet be discovered, and the inscriptions mentioned in the text brought to light.

TRANSLATION.

To the king, my lord, thy servant Ištar-dûrî ! Greeting to the king, my lord !

I send forthwith to my lord the king, in company with my messenger, the physicians Nabû-šum-iddina and Nabû-erba, of whom I spoke to the king, my lord. Let them be admitted to the presence of the king, my lord, and let the king, my lord, converse with them. I have not disclosed (to them) the true facts, but have told them nothing.[1] As the king, my lord, commands, (so) has it been done.

Šamaš-bel-uçur sends word from Der: "We have no inscriptions to place upon the temple walls." I send, therefore, to the king, my lord, (to ask) that one inscription be written out and sent immediately, (and that) the rest be speedily written, so that they may place them upon the temple walls.

There has been a great deal of rain, (but) the harvest is gathered. May the heart of the king, my lord, be of good cheer !

ACCENTED TRANSLITERATION.

[1]*Ana šarri belii̯a* [2]*ardúka Ištar-dûrî !*

[3]*Lû šulmu ana šarri belii̯a !*

[4]*Ina muxxi Nabû-šum-iddina* [5]*Nabû-erba, âse* [6]*ša ana šarri belii̯a* [7]*aqbûni, annûsim* [8][*itti?*] *apil-šiprî'a ina pân* [9]*šarri belii̯a assaprašunu.* [10]*Ina pân šarri belii̯a* [11]*lîrubû, šarru belî* [12]*issišunu lidbubu.* [13]*Kettu anâku* [14]*lâ ubarrî,* [15]*lâ aqabâšunu.* [16]*Bîd šarru belî išápar šaknúni.*

[17]*Šamaš-bel-uçur* [18]*ištu âl Deri issapra* [19]*mâ: "Muššarânî* (Edge) [20]*laššu, ina libbi igarâte.* (Rev.) [1]*ša bît-ili lâ niškun."* [2]*Umâ ana šarri belii̯a* [3]*assapra, išten muššarû* [4]*lišṭurû lušebilûni,* [5]*ina pitti rixûti* [6]*lišṭurû, ina libbi igarâte* [7]*ša bît-ili liškunû.*

[8]*Zunne ma'adâ* [9]*adanniš ittálak.* [10]*Ebûre deqi.* [11]*Libbi ša šarri belii̯a* [12]*lû ṭâbu.*

---

[1] Literally, "I have not disclosed the truth, not telling them" (circumstantial clause).

17.

K 660.

From a very early period the vine was successfully cultivated in Assyria, and the reports of modern travellers amply prove that the Rabshak of Sennacherib made no vain boast when he described his country to the Jews besieged within the walls of Jerusalem as "a land of corn and wine, a land of bread and vineyards, a land of olive trees and honey" (2 Kings xviii. 32; Isa. xxxvi. 17). Wine is frequently mentioned in the cuneiform inscriptions of Assyria and Babylonia, and was extensively used both for convivial purposes and in connection with religious ceremonies. Ašur-nâçir-pal (reigned 885–860 B. C.), for example, makes offerings of wine and fruit to the god Ašur and to the temples of his land, to celebrate the rebuilding of the city of Calah (*Asurn.*, iii. 135). Sennacherib (r. 705–681 B. C.), imposes upon the conquered Khirimme, an Aramean tribe of Babylonia, the payment of a tribute of wine to the gods of Assyria (*Prism*, i. 61). Nebuchadnezzar (r. 604–561 B. C.), the great Babylonian monarch who sacked Jerusalem and led away its inhabitants into captivity, offers annual apportionments of wine to his national gods (cf., e. g., *Nebuch. Grotefend*, ii. 32; iii. 15). And these are merely a few of the many instances that could be cited.

The ceremonial use of wine is depicted in sculpture, and frequently mentioned in the historical and in the religious texts. Thus, the liturgical text, K 164, referred to above, p. 154, directs, among other observances, the sprinkling of wine upon the couch of the god, and the pouring out of a libation upon the ground before it; Nabonidus, the last native king of Babylon (r. 555–538 B. C.) sprinkles with mead, wine, oil, and honey the temple of the Moon-god in Harran (V R 64, col. ii, 5); and in a sculpture from Nineveh, Sardanapallus (r. 668–626 B. C.) is represented in the act of pouring out a libation over the bodies of four lions that he has slain (Place, *Ninive et l' Assyrie*, Pl. 57; IR 7; cf. the frontispiece in Hommel's *Jagdinschriften*).

A reference to the use of wine on festal occasions is to be found in the fine address of the goddess Ištar to king Sardanapallus (Smith, *Asurb.*, p. 65, ll. 65–67), when, assuring him of her aid and protection against his enemy Teumman, king of Elam, she bids him, "eat food, drink wine, make music, while I go and accomplish this affair"; and the same Assyrian monarch is depicted in a beautiful sculpture (Place, *ibid.;* cf. Mürdter-Delitzsch², p. 139), seated, in company with his queen, under an arbor of grape-vines heavy with luscious clusters, surrounded by attendants, drinking wine from a richly chased goblet.

It is interesting to note in this connection that among the ten varieties of wine enumerated in a list published in the *Cuneiform Inscriptions of Western Asia* (ii. 44, 9–13), occurs the wine of Helbon, which is also mentioned by Ezekiel (xxvii. 18),[1] and that

---

[1] Cf. Cornill (p. 351) and Toy *ad loc.*

the same locality—the village of Khalbun, about nine miles north of Damascus—is noted for its vintage to the present day. The "receipt" of wine for the month of Ṭebet (January-February), spoken of in the following letter, was probably the produce of the royal vineyards for the preceding autumn, which, having undergone the necessary amount of fermentation and preparation, was now ready to be put up in leather bottles or casks,[1] and stored away for use. It is possible, however, that reference is had to a tax or tribute of wine, delivered in the month of Ṭebet. Of Bâbilâ, who with Bel-iqîša and another person whose name is obliterated, addresses the letter to the king, I am unable to give any information beyond the fact that his name means "the Babylonian," or rather "devoted to (the god of) Babylon"—a name like Arba'ilâ, "devoted to (Ištar of) Arbela," Mardukâ (Mordecai), "devoted to Merodach," etc.

To Bel-iqîša are ascribed two other letters published in Harper's work (No. 84=K 117, and No. 85=K 613). In the former the writer complains that, having addressed some remonstrances to the secretary of the palace, that official had made use of very energetic language to him, and had removed him from his post in the palace to another situation much less desirable. The second refers to three officers who have been promoted by the king, but whom their present commander refuses to release from his service that they may assume their new positions. Both these letters evidently proceed from the same person, and stamp the writer as what in American colloquial language would be termed "a kicker." Whether he was identical, however, with the Bel-iqîša of the present letter is not so certain. Several persons of this name occur in the epistolary texts, and any attempt at closer identification seems hazardous in this case. We need have little hesitation, however, in assuming that the communication was addressed to one of the Sargonide kings of Assyria. This letter, which is published in Harper's work (No. 86), conveys the information that the quantity of wine received in the month of Ṭebet is so great that the places of storage provided are entirely inadequate to contain it. It is therefore proposed to deposit it in the royal store-houses, which usually contained, we may suppose, only such wine as was specially selected and set apart for the king's private stock.

TRANSLATION.

To the king, our lord, thy servants . . . . . .,[2] Bel-iqîša, and Bâbilâ! Greeting to our lord the king! May Ašur, ... , Bel, and Nabû grant length of days for never-ending years to our lord the king!

---

[1] I prefer the former, and have so rendered, for reasons which will be given in the notes in Part II. Cf. meanwhile Delitzsch, *Handwörterbuch*, p. 354a.

[2] A name has been obliterated here.

The king, our lord, shall decide.[1] Since the receipt for the month Ṭebet is bottled,[2] and there are no places of shelter (for it), we would (wish to) put it into the royal store-houses for wine. Let our lord the king pass an order that the (proper store-)houses may be indicated to us, and we shall be relieved of embarrassment.[3] The wine of our lord the king is of great quantity; where shall we put it?

ACCENTED TRANSLITERATION.

[1]*Ana šarri belini,* [2]*ardânika . . . . . .* [3]*Bel-iqîša,* [4]*Bâbîlâ!*
[5]*Lû šulmu ana šarri* [6]*belini!*
Ašur, il . . . . . . [7]*Bel, Nabû ûme* [8]*arkûte šanâte* [9]*dârâte ana šarri* [10]*belini liddinû!*
[11]*Šarru belini* [12]*ûdâ. Kî* [13]*naxxartu ša arax Ṭebîti* [14]*karmatúni,* [15]*u çillâte* (Rev.) [1]*laššû, bîtâte-karâni* [2]*ša šarri belini nišâkanúni.* [3]*Šarru belini liqábî,* [4]*bîtâte lukallimûnâši, re[šni?]** [5]*niššî.* [6]*Karânu ša šarri* [7]*ma'ada, âka* [8]*niškun?*

18.

K 515.

From the earliest historical times to the present day, the navigation of the Tigris and the Euphrates has been conducted in essentially the same manner. The round, shallow vessels of plaited willow described by Herodotus (i. 194) are represented in the Assyrian sculptures, and are practically identical with the modern *kufa* which eastern travellers describe as being in common use upon both rivers. The *kelek* or raft with a frame work of wood supported by inflated skins, is also depicted in the sculptures, and is still extensively used, especially between Mosul and Bagdad. Starting with its freight from the former place, it floats down the rapid current of the Tigris, and on reaching its destination is broken up, the timber is sold, and the skins conveyed by camels or asses back to Mosul. Representations of ancient and modern keleks, and of the process of inflating the skins, may be seen in Place's *Ninive et l'Assyrie,* Pl. 43; (cf. Kaulen, *Assyr. und Babyl.*[4], p. 9) and an interesting account of

---

[1] I. e. whether it is proper that our intention shall be carried out.
[2] I. e. in leather bottles.
[3] Literally, "hold up our heads"; *niššî* is cohortative, as also *niškun* (l. 8); cf. Del., *Assyr. Gram.* § 145.
* Dr. Harper gives some traces which suggest the character *si*, but might also lend themselves to *iš*. *ni* seems to have been omitted by the scribe, owing to the following preformative *ni*.

these rafts is given in Layard's work, *Nineveh and its Remains* (i. ch. 13 ; ii. ch. 5).[1]

But, though extensively employed, as being well adapted to the Tigris, whose swift current offered a natural obstacle to upstream navigation, such clumsy rafts were by no means the only vessels with which the ancient Assyrians were acquainted. "Although," says Layard (*op. cit.*, ii. ch. 5), "the Assyrians were properly an inland people, yet their conquests and expeditions, particularly at a later period, brought them into contact with maritime nations. We consequently find, on the monuments of Khorsabad and Kouyunjik, frequent representations of naval engagements and operations on the sea-coast." Several illustrations of ancient vessels are to be found in the same work (ii. ch. 2 and 5). One of these, propelled by four oars on a side, has a single mast, at the top of which is a crow's nest, apparently for an archer or look-out. The mast is supported by fore and back-stays. Both prow and stern are very high, the former having the form of a horse's head, the latter that of the tail of a fish. In Place's *Ninive et l' Assyrie*, Pl. 50bis, a vessel of similar shape is represented following along the shore and picking up lions, which are driven by hunters from the brake into the water. This boat has two banks of oars, fifteen on each side, but no mast. Layard's *Monuments of Nineveh* presents (Pl. 71) illustrations of a number of vessels, evidently war-ships, having two banks of oars, and shields hanging along the bulwarks. Five have sheer prows and sharp beaks for ramming, and these have also a mast, a single yard, fore and back-stays, braces, and halliards. Ships are also frequently mentioned in the inscriptions, and an interesting text (K 4378) published in Delitzsch's *Lesestücke*[3] (pp. 86–90) contains an enumeration of different sorts of vessels and their parts. Mast, sails, yards, rudder, rigging, bulwarks, prow, stern, deck, hold, and keel are all mentioned ; and among the different kinds of vessels the "Assyrian ship" is specially designated, along with those of the Babylonian cities of Ur and Nippur. It is well known that the cuneiform account of the Deluge contains a detailed description of the building of the ship which the god Ea bade the Babylonian Noah construct.[2]

At the present day the Tigris is only navigable, even for vessels of light draught, up to about twenty miles below Mosul, and thence to Diarbekr only by raft, and it is doubtful whether the conditions were much more favorable in early times. As far as Bagdad, however, the river is navigable for light freight-bearing

---

[1] See also Rawlinson's *Herodotus*, Bk. i. c. 194, for valuable notes and references. Prof. Haupt has called my attention to an article in the *Daheim* of March 16th, 1895 (No. 24, p. 383[b] above), where it is stated that the African explorer Count Götzen, in the summer of 1894, crossed the rapid stream of the Lowa, a large tributary of the Congo, by means of a canoe and raft constructed of inflated goat skins. Consequently this species of raft seems not to have been confined to Mesopotamia.

[2] See Haupt's *Nimrod Epic*, p. 136, ll. 48 ff.

steamers, and it is possible that the vessels of the ancients may have been able to proceed even further up the stream.

Opis, where the writer of the letter translated below desired to establish a base of operations for his vessel, was an ancient commercial city of importance situated at the junction of the Tigris with the Adhem. It was conquered by Tiglathpileser I. about 1100 B. C.; and, continuing to flourish until a comparatively late period, is frequently mentioned by Greek writers (Herod., i. 189; Xen., *Anab.*, ii. 4, 25; Arrian, *Anab.*, vii. 7, 6; Strabo, ii. 1, 26; xi. 14, 8; xvi. 1, 9). Its ruins are still to be seen (cf. Delitzsch, *Paradies*, p. 205). It was to Opis that some of the ships built by Sennacherib in 696 or 695 B. C. for his expedition against Merodach-baladan were floated down the Tigris from Nineveh; starting thence, they sailed down the river to the district of Bît-Dakkûri, where they passed through the canal Arakhtu into the Euphrates, thus joining the rest of the fleet.[1] Bâb-bitqi was situated further down the Tigris. It is mentioned in a text of the time of Sargon (IV R², 46, no. 1, rev. 1) in connection with Bît-Dakkûri, which extended from the left bank of the Euphrates in the neighborhood of Babylon and Borsippa to the right bank of the Tigris. (Cf. Delitzsch, *Paradies*, p. 202.) It probably lay at the mouth of the canal Arakhtu mentioned above, which, crossing Bît-Dakkûri, passed through Babylon into the Euphrates, thus connecting the two great Mesopotamian rivers. *Bâb-bitqi* probably means *Gate* i. e. *Lock of the Cut* or *Ditch.*

Ṭâb-çil-Ešara ("Good is the shelter of Ešara"), the writer of the letter, was governor of the city of Aššur, and held the high office of eponym in the year 714 B. C. (Smith, *Eponym Canon*, p. 84). Thirteen of his letters are published in Harper's work (Nos. 87–99); and two others (R^M. 2, 458, 459) are edited by the same scholar in the *Zeitschrift für Assyriologie*, viii. pp. 355, 356, but most of them are unfortunately badly mutilated. One of them (K 507), which is also published in transliteration, with translation and commentary, by Delitzsch (*B.A.*, ii. p. 32),[2] refers to a certain Nabû-bel-šumâte, prefect of Bîrat, who being obliged to repel a raid upon Sippara, has been unable to present himself sooner before the king. Another (K 656=Harper, No. 92) gives an account of a large quantity of heavy timber for building purposes; and building operations in the city of Aššur are mentioned in K 5466 (=Harper, No. 99), rev. 6 ff., and in K 620 (=Harper, No. 91), rev. 2 ff.

A most important reference, which places beyond a doubt the identification of the writer with the eponym of the year 714 B. C., is contained in the former text (K 5466) ll. 6–9: "Since my lord the king has given freedom to the city of Aššur, and its

---

[1] See Prof. Haupt's paper on The Battle of Halûle, *Andover Review*, May, 1886, p. 543.

[2] Also by S. A. Smith in *PSBA.*, x. pt. 3, pl. ix., and pp. 173 ff.

government has devolved upon me, I am repairing the palace of the city of palaces."[1] King Sargon repeatedly mentions the fact that he restored to the cities of Aššur and Harran their ancient privileges and immunities, which had long fallen into abeyance (cf. Winckler's *Keilschrifttexte Sargons*, pp. 80, 96, 146, 158, 174); and the building operations mentioned by Ṭâb-çil-Ešara were doubtless due to the desire of the Assyrian monarch to restore to the former capital of his empire something of its pristine glory. Ṭâb-çil-Ešara, who was governor of Aššur under Sargon (r. 722–705 B. C.), may well have lived on into the reign of Sargon's son and successor Sennacherib (r. 705–681 B. C.), and therefore it is not impossible that the ships mentioned in the letter may have constituted part of the fleet built by the latter monarch in 696–695. There is no record of the possession by the Assyrians of a permanent navy, and these vessels, having served the purpose for which they were constructed, may well have been either broken up or acquired by individuals for commercial purposes.

The following letter, which is so clear as to need no special explanation, would seem to show that Opis was considered a more desirable point for operating freight vessels than Bâb-bitqi. It is published in Harper's *Letters*, No. 89, and may be translated as follows:

TRANSLATION.

To the king, my lord, thy servant Tâb-çil-Ešara!

Greeting to the king, my lord!

May Ašur and Belit bless the king, my lord!

That ship of mine in which the grand vizier conveyed money down (the river), is now stopping at Bâb-bitqi, and the ship of the governor of Arrapakhitis is carrying on a ferry at Opis. My lord the king shall decide. We transport in her straw, fodder, (and) such matters. (?)

Let now the ship of the governor of Arrapakhitis come and carry on a ferry at Bâb-bitqi, and let mine go to Opis so that we may transport straw and fodder in her (there). The men of the governor of Arrapakhitis are already conducting a ferry at Bâb-bitqi.

ACCENTED TRANSLITERATION.

[1]*Ana šarri beliįa,* [2]*ardûka Ṭâb-çil-Ešara!*

[3]*Lû šulmu ana šarri beliįa!*

[4]*Ašur, Belit ana šarri beliįa* [5]*likrubû!*

[6]*Elippu šî įâtu,* [7]*abarakku kaspu ina libbi* [8]*usserida,* [9]*ina Bâb-bitqi* [10]*tâzâza,* [11]*u elippu ša paxâti* [12]*ša Arapxa ina libbi Upî'a* [13]*nîburu tuppaš.* [14]*Šarru belu ûdâ.* [15]*Nîni* (?) *tibnu*

[1] Or the city of Ekallâti. See *Sennach. Bavian*, 48–50.

kisûtu [16]*dibbâte*(?) *ammêti* (?) [17]*nuše[bar ina libbiša]*. (Rev.) [1]*[Umâ at]â elippu* [2]*ša paxâti ša Arapxa* [3]*lû tallik*, [4]*ina Bâb-bitqi* [5]*nîburu lû tuppiš*, [6]*u ịâtu lû tallika*, [7]*ina Upî'a* [8]*tibnu kisûtu* [9]*ina libbiša nušebira.* [10]*Çâbê ša paxâti* [11]*ša Arapxa* [12]*ina Bâb-bitqi* [13]*nîburu* [14]*uppušû.*

19.

K 1274.

Since all, or nearly all, the Assyro-Babylonian epistolary texts that have as yet been found are those which were stored up in royal palaces among the archives, letters of an official character constitute, as may be supposed, by far the greater number. But few letters of private individuals have been discovered, and those of women, of whatever rank, are extremely rare. In fact, I am only acquainted with two, and it is interesting to note that both are characteristic.

One of these, from an Assyrian princess,[1] a grand-daughter of Sardanapallus, conveys a rebuke to a presumptuous court lady who has been guilty of a flagrant breach of etiquette. The other, from a woman whose social status is not evident, contains an appeal in behalf of some unfortunate slaves who have claimed her intercession. She bears the name of *Sa-ra-a-a*, that is *Sarâ'a.*[2] One is naturally tempted to compare this name to *Sarai* (שָׂרַי), the by-form of *Sarah* (שָׂרָה). *Sarâ'a* would then have to be, not an Assyrian, but a Jewish name borrowed from Hebrew. The genuine Assyrian equivalent of Sarah (שָׂרָה) is, of course, *Šarratu* 'queen,' but in foreign words Hebrew שׂ or שׁ is rendered by *s* in Assyrian.[3]

The letter probably dates from the Sargonide period; and the fact that the Assyrian and not the Babylonian character is employed, as well as the title of the official to whom it is addressed, would indicate that it proceeds from an Assyrian city which contained a royal residence (Nineveh, Calah, Aššur, etc.). It is, of course, impossible to define the relations existing between Sarâ'a and the royal secretary; she was possibly his wife or a lady of his harem, and certainly one who either had or was supposed to have influence with him.

The slaves appear to have been conveyed, at some previous time, to the governor of Bît-Na'âlâni, whether by gift or purchase is not stated. The governor sold them to a certain Marduk-

[1] Translated, with transliteration and commentary, by the present writer in *Johns Hopkins University Circulars*, No. 126 (June 1896), pp. 91–93.

[2] Cf. *Zeitschrift für Assyriologie*, ii. p. 260 below.

[3] See *Johns Hopkins University Circulars*, August, 1887, p. 118[b].

erba, and they, having reason to object to or dread this arrangement, applied to Sarâ'a, begging her to use her influence with their former master to prevent the consummation of the bargain, perhaps by repurchasing them. The officer who had executed the bill of sale on the part of the governor was with them, ready, apparently, to hand them over to the purchaser in case their appeal failed, so that prompt action in the matter was necessary.

The letter, which is published in Harper's *Letters*, No. 220, may be thus translated :

TRANSLATION.

To my lord, the secretary of the palace, thy handmaid Sarâ'a ! May Bel, Belit, ... ,[1] Belit of Babylon, Nabû, Tašmet, Ištar of Nineveh, and Ištar of Arbela bless my lord ! May they grant my lord long life with health of mind and body !

The governor of Bît-Na'âlâni has sold to Marduk-erba the slaves—seven in number—whom he had from my lord. These people are now here, (and) have come to me, saying, "Inform the secretary of the palace, before we are conveyed to the house of Marduk-erba." My lord, the officer who executed the contract is now with them.

ACCENTED TRANSLITERATION.

[1]*Ana dupšar ekalli, beli̯i̯a,* [2]*amtúka Sarâ'a !*

[3]*Bel, Belit, ... Belit Bâbîli,* [4]*Nabû, Tašmetu*[m], *Ištar ša Ninua,* [5]*Ištar ša Arba'il ana beli̯i̯a* [6]*likrubû !*

Ûme arkûti ṭûb libbi [7]*ṭûb šîre ana beli̯i̯a liddinû !*

[8]*Ardâni ša beli̯i̯a,* [9]*ša paxâtu ša Bît-Na'âlâni* (Rev.) [1]*iššû*—VII *napšâte šunu*—[2]*ana Marduk-erba ittedinšunu.* [3]*Annûšim nîše annaka šunu,* [4]*ittalkûnu ina muxxi̯i̯a* [5]*mâ : "Ina pâni dupšar ekalli qibî"*—[6]*mâ : "adâ bît Marduk-erba* [7]*lâ ušerabanâšina."*

[8]*Rešu, belî, iqnuqúni,* [9]*annûšim issišunu.*

20.

K 1239.

The text of this letter is published in Harper's *Letters*, No. 219, and in Winckler's *Sammlung von Keilschrifttexten*, ii. p. 48. It is written in the cursive Babylonian character, and the mention of Ezida ("the true house"), the celebrated temple of the god Nabû in Borsippa, would seem to leave little doubt as to the locality whence it proceeded. For the date, there is not sufficient evidence. The writer Bel-upâq ("Bel gives heed"),

---

[1] The name of another god has been obliterated here.

after the usual formula of greeting, informs his father that he has consulted the oracle in regard to a projected undertaking, and that the god has fixed upon the fourth day of the month as the most favorable occasion for entering upon it. All the necessary arrangements have been made, and the overseer, to whom the conduct of the work is to be entrusted, is fully instructed as to the bearing of the oracle, so that he may know how to select such modes of procedure as may be lucky, and avoid all that is unlucky. The letter may be translated as follows :

TRANSLATION.

Letter of Bel-upâq to Kunâ his father !

Greeting to my father !

I pray daily to Nabû and Nanâ for my father's life, and I pay heedful reverence to Ezida in thy behalf. When I consulted the god of the temple in regard to thee, he fixed upon the fourth of the month as the propitious occasion. Thy workmaster is fully instructed in regard to every matter so far as his (the god's) words are propitious.

ACCENTED TRANSLITERATION.

[1]*Duppu Bel-upâq* [2]*ana Kunâ abišu !*

[3]*Lû šulum ana abii̯a !*

[4]*Ûmussu Nabû u Nanâ* [5]*ana balâṭ napšâte ša abii̯u* [6]*uçallî, u ilku* [7]*ana Ezida* [8]*ana muxxika* [9]*kunnâk.*

[10]*Ilu mâr bîti** *ana* [11]*muxxika* (Edge) [12]*kî* [13]*aš'alu,* (Rev.) [1]*adannu ša šulum* [2]*adî ûmi rebî iççabta.* [3]*Ana mimma kalâma,* [4]*mala dibbušu* [5]*šulum, ummânka* [6]*xussu.*

---

* A god *Mâr-bîti* seems to be mentioned III R 66, 11 b. rev., but this may be merely an epithet like other names in the same column. It seems better to read as above.

THE EPISTOLARY LITERATURE

OF THE

ASSYRIANS AND BABYLONIANS

BY

CHRISTOPHER JOHNSTON

Johns Hopkins University

Baltimore, Md.

PART II.

The Epistolary Literature of the Assyrians and Babylonians. —By Dr. Christopher Johnston, Johns Hopkins University, Baltimore, Md.

PART II.[1]

Notes and Glossary to the Selected Letters.

As stated in Part I. of this paper (vol. xviii. p. 129, n. 2), the third and fourth volumes of Harper's excellent *Corpus Epistolarum* appeared while my article was going through the press. All the texts I have treated are, therefore, now readily accessible to scholars ;[2] and, in view of the fact that accented transliterations have already been given in Part I., while syllabic transliterations of all the words which occur in them are given in the subjoined Glossary, it seems superfluous to publish these texts in syllabic transliteration, as was done by Delitzsch in his series of papers on Assyrian Epistolary Literature in the *Beiträge zur Assyriologie.* Nor has it seemed necessary, in the present state of Assyriology, to give any extensive philological commentary. Philological explanations have, so far as possible, been relegated to the Glossary, where they can be given in the most convenient form ; the Glossary is, in fact, intended to supply all that is needful in this direction, and at the same time to serve as a commentary. The following notes have, therefore, been directed chiefly to the explanation of the more difficult syntactical constructions, to notices of previous translations of some of the texts, and to some general remarks in regard to the subject matter of certain passages. In the Glossary a strictly alphabetical arrangement has been adopted, which will, it is hoped, be sufficiently clear to require no explanation. It may, however, be well to note that if two words have the same consonantal skeleton, the forms with short vowels precede those with long vowels, and the forms with simple consonants those with doubled consonants ; for instance,

---

[1] For Part I. see vol. xviii., 1897, pp. 125–175.

[2] The following texts in Part I. are now published in Harper's work : 1 (K 524) = H. 282 ; 2 (K 13) = H. 281 ; 3 (K 10) = H. 280 ; 4 (K 528) = H. 269 ; 5 (K 79) = H. 266 ; 6 (K 824) = H. 290 ; 14 (S 1064) = H. 392.

adu, idu, udu ; âdu, îdu, ûdu, êdu ; adû, idû, udû ; âdû, îdû, ûdû, êdû ; addu, iddu, uddu ; addû, iddû, uddû. Compare my review of Delitzsch's *Assyrisches Handwörterbuch* in the American Journal of Philology, vol. xvii. pp. 485–491.

Notes.

i. (*K 524.*)

l. 8. S. A. Smith and Strassmaier read the second character in this line DAM, i. e. *aššatu ;* Pinches and Harper NIN, i. e. *axâtu.*

ll. 9–11. *ultu . . . ittalka.* Strassmaier (S. A. Smith, *Asurbanipal,* ii. p. 87) renders: "von Elam aus ist in Gefangenschaft gerathen ; zu den Tachâ war er (gegangen=) gebracht worden," which can hardly be reconciled with the text.

ll. 11–12. *ultu . . . açbata.* Smith :[1] "als ich seine Hände von den Tachâ zurück erhielt." What this means it is difficult to say.

l. 14. Smith reads here *adî napšâtešu,* taking ME as = MEŠ, and translates, "noch am Leben." Pinches (p. 77) correctly *zi-me.*

l. 17. Smith: "es war ein Bote da," but *ibášû* would have to be the present, "there *is* a messenger." In this case, moreover, we should expect *ibášî,* and it seems better to read *ibâšu* "has come to him." Smith has also failed to understand the conjunctional use of *ša* in this line.

l. 19. Smith reads *Ti-il-*[*mu-un*], but the traces as given both by Harper and by Smith himself, hardly favor this restoration.

l. 22. Strassmaier (p. 87) : "fragten um ein Orakel."

l. 26. Smith : "50 Stück Kleider," taking KU = *çubâtu.* KU is certainly obscure here, but it can hardly stand for *çubâtu.*

l. 27. *ana kaspi ina qâtišu itabkûni.* Smith : "mit Silber gaben sie in seine Hände." For this phrase, which often occurs in the contract tablets, cf. Tc 30, sub אבך.

l. 29. *immereni* 'our sheep.' Smith reads *lu ardá-ni,* and translates 'Hausschafe.' Of course LU-NITA is merely the common ideogram for *immeru,* and *ni* is the pronominal suffix. For Strassmaier's singular rendering of ll. 29 ff., which Smith, in spite of some objections, considers "sehr passend," cf. Smith ii. p. 88. It is hardly worth while to reproduce it here.

l. 31. *sâdu:* Smith compares *sa-a-du = na-a-ru,* V R. 28, 1 ef., which Strassmaier renders "Ufer des Flusses"; but cf. *HW.,*

---

[1] Wherever Smith is cited in these notes, S. A. Smith is meant.

p. 488ᵃ. In this line Smith translates *šâdu* 'Ufer(?)', in l. 39, 'Grenze(?).'

2. (*K. 13.*)

ll. 1–7. These lines, of which the beginnings are mutilated, may be readily restored, partly by comparing them with K 10 (H. 280), ll. 1–4, and partly from the context. In l. 5, we must evidently restore [DIŠ *Um-ma-xal-d*]*a-a-šu;* in l. 6, [*i-tu-ra*]*-am-ma* is required by the context; and in l. 7, the restoration *ki-*[*i ip*]*-la-xu* is obvious.

l. 14. *šaknû, iqábû*, circumstantial, § 152. *Umma* here refers to the whole of what follows, and this contains two separate quotations, each introduced by *kî*.

ll. 16–18. For my former reading of these lines (vol. xviii. p. 141) I would substitute the following: [16]*Agâ gabbi ina puluxti ša emûqu ša* [17]*bel šarrâni belija. Mât Elamti kîma de'i xurrurû,* [18]*marušti itûrû, puluxti ulteribû,* "all these parts are in terror of the troops of the lord of kings, my lord. The Elamites are ravaged as though (by) a plague, they are in a state of utter calamity, they are invaded by panic." *Mât Elamti* stands here figuratively for the Elamites, and hence the use of the plural, as constructio ad sensum, in the verbs that follow.—*marušti itûrû*, properly "they have turned into, become, calamity"; cf. אני שלום "I am (all) peace," Ps. cxx. 7, אני תפלה "I am (all) prayer," Ps. cix. 4. For examples of *târu* meaning 'to become,' cf. *HW.*, p. 702ᵃ.—*puluxti ulteribû*, properly "they have been caused to get into a panic."

l. 20. Delitzsch, *HW.*, p. 362ᵃ, gives *kutallu* without translation, but I see no reason for departing from the generally accepted rendering 'side,' which is supported by all the passages in which the word occurs (cf. *HW.*, l. c.; *B.A.*, i. p. 227). Cf. כתל, Cant. ii. 19; כתל, Dan. v. 5; כְּתָלַיָּא, Ezr. v. 8, 'wall,' i. e. properly side of a house or room; Syr. כותלא 'poop, stern' of a vessel, where it is limited by usage to the rear side.—*muššurat* means not "was abandoned" (im Stich gelassen, *HW.*, p. 362ᵃ), but, as formerly rendered by Delitzsch (B.A. i. p. 227), "was let loose, fell away." For *muššuru* as a synonym of Heb. שלח, cf. Haupt's remarks in PAOS., March, '94, p. cvii. The sense of the passage is that, when famine was added to the many evils under which the land already labored, there was a general defection from the party of Ummanaldas, and factional spirit was rife. Some parts of Elam, indeed, were in a state of open revolt, alleging as a pretext their dissatisfaction at the slaying of Umkhulumâ (ll. 21–23). The words *mâtsunu gabbi ina kutallišunu muššurat*, "their whole land fell away from their side," lead naturally to what follows.

l. 26. Literally, "is not this the word which," etc.?—*adî lâ axâliqu*, the present is here employed as the tense of incomplete action.

l. 35. *paširâti* "as a guarantee, credentials." Bel-ibnî proposes to arrange for the capture of Nabû-bel-šumâte by sending a private message to Ummanaldas, with the royal signet to serve as credentials and to lend force to his request, or rather command. He fears, however, that Sardanapallus may deem such a method beneath his dignity, and may prefer to send his command, in the usual manner, by a royal courier. That—the king may think—will be credentials enough for the Elamites. But Ummanaldas, however willing he may be, is weak, and Nabû-bel-šumâte, being not only exceedingly wary, but possessing, moreover, great influence with the Elamite nobles, can easily make himself secure by the judicious use of money, if once he gets wind of the affair. The arrival of the royal messenger, accompanied by an escort of soldiers, will be sure to attract his attention and to arouse his suspicion. It is best, therefore, to use less open means, and perhaps, if only the gods will be active in the matter, the wily Chaldean may yet be taken unawares and delivered over to the Assyrian king.

l. 46. *ultu Umxulumâ' balṭu*, properly, "from, commencing from (the time that), U. was alive."

ll. 47 ff. It had been the habit of Nabû-bel-šumâte to lavish his portion upon his partizans, but now times are hard and grain is scarce. He therefore alleges that the officers who controlled the distribution of the grain had defrauded him of his proper share, and claims restitution. Accordingly he seizes every šarnuppu he can catch and compels him to hand over the original amount claimed, together with an enormous increase by way of interest and indemnity. Ummanaldas, who naturally objects to these proceedings, sends several times to demand the surrender of the grain thus seized, but without success.

3. (*K 10.*)

l. 8. *kâdu:* the meaning 'post, garrison,' seems to suit the context. The general sense is clear. The Assyrians, under command of Mušezib-Marduk (rev. 2. 12), were to use Sabdânu as a base of operations, and thence to harrass the Elamites.

l. 17. *qaqqar ina pânišunu rûqu* "a long stretch of ground lay before them." The small force of five hundred men operating in a hostile country, where they were constantly liable to attack, could hardly undertake a long march encumbered by a large number of prisoners, and for this reason more than two hundred had to be put to death.

ll. 24–25. *pîšunu iddanûnu*, literally, "they gave their utterance," i. e. they sent a message to arrange the terms (*ade*) of capitulation.

4. (*K 528.*)

l. 9. *tušaçbat-ma*, here with ellipsis of *xarrânu*, as indicated by *tašápar* which follows (l. 10). For the expression *xarrânu çabâtu, suçbutu*, cf. *HW.*, pp. 561[a], 562[a].

l. 13. *mât Elamti ildudá-ma.* For my former rendering of these words (vol. xviii. p. 145), I would substitute, "brought Elam (against us)." Cf. *nakru u bûbûti ina muxxi bît belika ul tašdud* "thou hast not brought foe or famine against thy lord's house," 6, 27–29.—l. 22. For *attallak* (vol. xviii. p. 146) read *adálap.*

ll. 29–32. *nipxur-ma, nillik-ma, nuterá-ma, niddin,* are all cohortatives (§ 145).

5. (*K 79.*)

l. 7. In the name *Pir'i-Bel,* the original has, instead of DINGIR-EN, I-*en* (i. e. *išten*), which is doubtless a mere scribal error. I assume that the published text is correct as Pinches (IV R.[2], 46) and Harper (No. 266) agree.

l. 8. *šanâte agâ* x, literally, these ten years.

Rev. ll. 18-19 (=II. 266, r. 13–14). The text of these lines seems to be very uncertain (cf. Bezold, *Literatur*, p. 240). The following *šunûti-ma . . . liqbû* would seem to indicate that proper names preceded.

6. (*K 824.*)

l. 5. Note *ša tašpur* here and in l. 35 without the overlapping vowel. S. A. Smith has entirely misunderstood the passage that follows.

ll. 17–20. The construction of these lines offers some difficulty. It seems best to take *ul* as used absolutely 'No!' and *ina* . . . *qatâta* as parenthetical. Ordinarily we should expect *â âmur* in l. 20, but the negation has already been expressed by *ul*, and it is not necessary to repeat it. This loose construction is due to the insertion of *ina* . . . *qatâta*, which interrupts the continuity. Smith renders: "Du bist nicht wegen des Dienstes des Hauses deines Herrn getrennt," etc.

l. 29. Smith reads *ultušdud*, but the usual form would be *ultašdid*, and the context requires the second person.

l. 36. *ban ša tepušâ* "the good (service) which ye have done." *ban* is construct (before the relative) of *banû*, 'honorable, good,' etc. Cf. *ba-ni ša tašpura* "it is well that thou hast sent," K. 95 (H. 288), r. 3; *ba-ni ša taçbatâšunûti* "it is well that ye have seized them," K. 94 (H. 287), 7. Cf. also *banû* in l. 39 of the present text.

8. (*K 629.*)

Rev. l. 6. *nâš-šappâte* is nominative absolute.—*ša niqûšu ibâšûni*, literally, "(he) whose offering exists."

l. 13. *lušallimû lîpušû* "may they perfectly execute," like Heb. ויסף ויקח אשה, Arab. ما عاد رجع, etc.

9. (*K. 547.*)

l. 1. *dupšar mâti.* The traces given by Harper, and the following *mâti* (cf. W. 24) shows that A-BA is to be restored here. Delitzsch (*HW.*, p. 4[a]) gives A-BA without translation, and refers to *dupšarru*, where, however, no mention of A-BA is to be found. In his *Wörterbuch* (p. 23) A-BA is fully discussed, but is not connected with *dupšarru*. In a note on K. 572, 6 (*B.A.*, i. p. 218) he gives *dupšarru* as the equivalent of the ideogram A-BA, and points out the interchange between A-BA and *dupšarru* in III R. 2, Nos. iii, vii, xiii; 64, 35b. In III R. 2, Marduk-šum-iqîša, father of Nabû-zuqup-kena, is designated, ll. 17. 22. 24. 38. 55, as [amel] DUB-SAR, or, ll. 2. 8. [amel] DUB-SAR-RIM, while in ll. 2. 9, and III R. 64, 35b, he bears the title of [amel] A-BA. In Knudtzon's *Gebete an den Sonnengott*, No. 109, 9, we find [*lû* [amel] DUB-SAR-]MEŠ *Aššurâ lû* [amel] DUB-SAR-MEŠ *Armâ*, which may be compared with [amel] A-BA *Aššurâ*, [amel] A-BA *Armâ* II R. 31, 64. 65. Further, in a large number of passages in the contract tablets we find the [amel] A-BA exercising the legal or notarial functions of the *dupšarru* (cf. W. 23). In view of these facts I have here, and in 19, 1, rendered A-BA by *dupšarru.* I have done so, however, with a certain reservation. While I believe that A-BA can in general be replaced by *dupšarru,* it is by no means certain that it is merely ideogram for *dupšarru.* Of course, A-BA must not be confounded with AB-BA explained by *šîbu* 'old man, elder'; but it is entirely possible that A-BA had some similar meaning, and was applied to the *dupšarru* as a term of respect, in the same way that *sheikh* is used in Arabic. It is a fact worthy of notice that in K.B. iv. we find in the Assyrian legal documents, from Rammân-nirarî III to Ašurbanipal, invariably A-BA, never *dupšarru,* while in Babylonian tablets of a similar character *dupšarru* (amel DUB-SAR, amel ŠID) consistently occurs from Šumu-abim (p. 10, l. 25) to Antiochus III (p. 319, l. 25), never A-BA; and Tallqvist, in his *Sprache der Contracte Nabû-nâ'id's,* does not mention A-BA as occurring in any Babylonian contract. Moreover, in Babylonian tablets, dated in the reign of the Assyrian king Sin-šar-iškun, we find, not A-BA, but *dupšarru.* Cf. K. B., iv. p. 174, Nos. i. ii. (dated at Sippar); 176, No. iii. (dated at Uruk). In the earlier Babylonian documents (K.B., iv. pp. 1–48) we find invariably amel DUB-SAR, while later amel ŠID seems to be most commonly used.

14. (*S 1064.*)

ll. 9–11. S. A. Smith renders: "um die allgemeine Entzündung zu vermindern die um seine Augen ist," which needs no comment. *Sikru* stands for *zikru* 'man'; for similar interchange in case of the homonym *zikru* 'name, command,' cf. *sikir šaptišu,* Asurn. i. 5, *sikir pîja,* Lay. 43, 2, *sikir Šamaš* Tig. Pil. i. 31. I see no necessity to assume, with Delitzsch (*HW.,* pp. 254^b, 510^a), the existence of two stems זכר and סקר. There is no evidence for the occurrence of ק in this stem except when followed by *u,* and in this case *qu* is merely a phonetic spelling, indicating the sound of the consonant as modified by the vowel following.

l. 14. Smith takes *irtumu* as $\mathfrak{Q}^t$ of רום. I prefer to take it as prt. of רתם; see the glossary. For the use of the *modus relativus* without *ša* cf. § 147, 2.

ll. 24 ff. *ilânika* is nominative absolute.

l. 31. Smith: "noch 7 oder 8 Tage wird er leben," which is exactly the opposite of the true sense.

15. (*K 519.*)

Rev. l. 6. *ma'adu*, not adjective, but noun in apposition to *dâme;* literally, "blood, a (multitude, that is, a) profusion."

l. 10. *naxnaxete ša appi* can only mean the alæ of the nose, as is shown by the context. Plugging the nares had not hitherto been resorted to, for that is the remedy suggested by Arad-Nanâ. The treatment must therefore have consisted in the application of external compresses, which could only have been placed upon (*ina muxxi*, l. 9) the alæ. In such a case the nasal breathing would be impeded by the compresses, while, unless skilfully applied, the bandages, required to keep them in place, would interfere with breathing by the mouth.

l. 11. *naxnaxûtu* 'breathing': this rendering suits the context, and is also suggested by *naxnaxete* (properly 'breathers') in the preceding line.

l. 12–13. *ištu pâni dâme uçûni* "the blood flows in spite (of them)," literally "from before (them)"; that is, they only serve to interfere with the breathing of the patient, and do not check the hemorrhage (cf. r. ll. 3–7).—*šunu*, referring to *lippe*, is to be understood after *ina pâni;* cf. *ina libbi* used similarly without the pronominal suffix, 14, 25.

16. (*K 504.*)

l. 12. *lidbubu*. We should, of course, expect *lidbub; lid-bu-bu* may be a mere scribal error due to the influence of *li-ru-bu* in the preceding line.

l. 13. *kettu* (*ki-e-tu*). S. A. Smith renders 'faithfully(?)' and connects with what precedes. In a note he states that he is "not certain as to the meaning and derivation of this word."

l. 16. Smith: "the house of the king, my lord sent to me."

Rev. ll. 5–6. *ina . . . lišṭurû*. Smith renders: "suddenly they were destroyed; may they be written."(!)

ll. 8–10. *zunnu, ebûru;* the sign MEŠ is here not plural, but collective. Note the singular verbs. Smith: "Much rain constantly shall come. May the harvest (when) threshed the heart of the king, my lord, rejoice."

17. (*K 660.*)

l. 14. *karmatûni;* 3 fem. permans. agreeing with *naxxartu*. Strassmaier, *Nbn.*, No. 386 is an account of the receipt of 34 *na-ak-ri-ma-nu* (l. 14), which were made of leather, as shown by the determinative SU (= *mašak*) ll. 1. 4., and served *ana ki-ri-mu ša šikar* ŠE-BAR (ll. 1. 2.), and *ana ki-ri-mu silqâtu u šikar* ŠE-BAR (ll. 11–12). *šikar* ŠE-BAR, i. e. drink prepared from grain, must certainly mean 'beer.' *silqu*, which occurs in a list of plants and vegetables explained by Meissner (*Z.A.*, vi. pp. 289 ff.) means 'beet,' and corresponds to Aram. סילקא (*Z.A.*, vi. p. 295; T[c] 111). In the passage before us *silqâtu* (*si-il-qa-a-tu*) may be simply the fem. pl. of *silqu* (cf. *šumu*, pl. *šumâte*), or, as it occurs here with *šikaru*, it may be the name of a fermented liquor prepared from beet juice. It is difficult to see what objects of leather could have been used in this connection except the skins in which the beer and beet wine (or beets, in which case the skins would be used as bags) were contained. The words *nakrimânu ana kirema ša šikar* ŠE-BAR may therefore be rendered "leather bottles for bottling beer." Meissner (l. c.) compares *kirimmu* 'womb.' Taking into consideration the analogy of *ummu*, the stem כרם might well mean 'to be capacious,' and so 'to contain,' etc. For these reasons I have rendered *karmatûni* 'is bottled,' which suits the context well.

Glossary.

א

u (ו, و) *and:* (1) connecting nouns ṭûb libbi u ṭûb šîri *health of mind and body* I, 4–5; (2) connecting verbs ilu ušeçâ u ussaxxar *he will carry the god forth and bring him back* 8, r. 2–3.—Adversative, *but:* u Ašur . . . urâqâni *but A. withholds me* 6, 12; u ina libbi ša *but because*, etc., 6, 23.—(HW 1[a])

a'âdu (ועד ?).—𝔖 *to apply, have recourse, to* (properly *to make an appointment*, הועיד): kî tuše'idâ (tu-še-i-da) *when ye applied* 2, 54; kî uše'iduš (u-še-'-i-du-uš) *although he has applied for it* 2, 59.—(HW 230[a])

abu (אב, أب) *father:* abija (AD-ja) *my father* 4, 14; 6, 15; 20, 3. 5; a-bu-šu 5, 15, a-bi-šu 5, 9. 11, AD-šu 20, 2 *his father;* axe abišu (AD-šu) *his uncles* 3, 15.—(W 17; HW 3[a])

abâku (prop. *to turn* = הפך, in which פ is due to a partial assimilation of ב to כ) *to bring, carry off, purchase.*—𝔔[1] ana kaspi ina qâtišu îtabkûni (i-tab-ku-ni) *they purchased from him* 1, 27 ; cf. T[c] 30.—(W 28; HW 6[a])

abâlu (יבל), prt. ûbil, prs. ubbal, *to bring.*—Š *to send, convey:* 1 pl. nušebila (nu-še-bi-la) 5, r. 13. 24; 3 pl. ušebilû-ni (u-še-bi-lu-[ni]) 3, r. 14. Prec. 1 sg. lušebiluní-ma (lu-še-bi-lu-nim-ma) 2, 34 ; lušebil (lu-še-bil) 2, 36; 3 pl. lušebilûni (lu-še-bil-u-ni) 16, r. 4.—Š[t] *same*, 1 sg. ussébila (u-si-bi-la) 10, r. 4 ; § 51, 2.—(HW 230[a])

ubânu (אבן,) *finger:* ubâni (šu-si) çixirti *the little finger* 14, 23.—(W 41 ; HW 8[b])

ebêru (עבר), prt. ebir, prs. ibbir, *to cross.*—Q[t] etébir (i-te-bir) *he crossed* (the river) 2, 10.—Š *to convey over, transport:* nušebar (nu-še-[bar]) *we transport* 18, 17 ; nušebira (nu-še-bi-ra) *let us transport* (cohort.) 18, r. 9.—(W 59 ; HW 10[b])

ebûru (עֲבוּר) *harvest:* ebûru-meš 16, r. 10 (where the plural sign merely emphasizes the collective meaning of the noun).—(W 66 ; HW 11[b])

abarakku, an official title, *grand vizier:* [amel]abarakku (ši-dub) 18, 7.—(W 68 ; HW 12[a])

agâ *this, these*, for all genders, numbers, and cases; written a-ga-a 2, 16. 48; 4, 24; 6, 20, etc.; a-ga-ia 2, 26.—(W 76 ; HW 13[b])

igaru (אגר,, جدر) *wall:* pl. igarâte (e-libit-meš) 16, 20. r. 6.—(W 105 ; HW 18[b])

egirtu (אגרת) *letter:* e-gir-tu 4, 36.—(W 103 ; HW 18[a])

idu (יד, يد, Eth. *ĕd*) *hand:* idâšu (id[2]-šu) *his hands* (preceded by determ. uzu, i. e. šîru) 14, 25. Pl. idâte (i-da-te), but in what sense? 15, 12.—(HW 303[a])

adû (עד, עֲדֵי), usually in genit. adî, properly *continuance, duration.*—(1) a-du-u *now*, 3, r. 22.—(2) *during, within*, a-du ûme vii viii ibálaṭ *he will be well in 7 or 8 days* 14, 31.—(3) *as soon as*, a-di 1, 14.—(4) *until*, a-di 5, r. 13; 7, r. 17; 20, r. 2.—(5) *as far as* (of space) ultu . . . adî (a-di) *from . . . to* 2, 49; 3, r. 18–19.—(6) adî(û) lâ (followed by prs.) *before*, a-di lâ 2, 26; a-du-u lâ 19, r. 6–7.—(W 127 ; HW 22[b]. 24[a])

adû (ודא) prt. ûdî, prs. ûdâ, *to determine, decide:* šarru beli (belu) ûdâ (u-da) *the king shall decide* 7, r. 19; 8, 11 ; 17, 12 ; 18, 14.—(HW 232[a])

adû (properly infin. of preceding) *statute, law, compact:* ade (a-di-e)... iççab'tû *they made terms* **3**, 25; kî adî (a-di) *according to compact* **1**, 28.—(HW 232[b])

idû (ידע), prt. and prs. îdî, *to know.*—Prs. 1 sg. mod. rel. îdû (i-du-u) **6**, 24; 3 pl. îdû (i-du-u) **4**, 11. Prec. 3 sg. lû îdî (i-di) **5**, r. 27.—(HW 303[a])

adannu (=adânu, ועד?) *time, period:* a-dan-nu ša šulum *the propitious time* **20**, r. 1.—(W 135; HW 26[b])

adanniš, addanniš (=ana danniš) *greatly, exceedingly:* a-dan-niš **7**, 4; **10**, 4; **12**, r. 6; **16**, r. 9; ad-dan-niš **14**, 3. 8. 28; **15**, 3. 7.—(W 160; HW 26[b]; Hebraica x. 196).

adru, perhaps *enclosure* (חדר): ad-ri ekalli *the palace enclosure* **8**, 15. 16. (Cf. adûru *enclosure,* HW 29[b])

idâte, see idu.

idatûtu, perhaps *confirmation, ratification,* of a bargain or agreement: ana i-da-tu-tu *to bind the bargain*(?) **1**, 26. (Cf. T[c] 76, sub יד)

ezêbu (עזב), prt. ezib, prs. izzib, *to leave:* Š[t] *to save, rescue:* usezibû (u-si-zi-bu) *they rescued* **7**, r. 4.—(§ 51, 2; W 244; HW 34[b])

axu (אח, أخ) *brother:* axija (šEš-ia) *my brother* **6**, 34; axušu (šEš-šu) ša *the brother of* **7**, 14; axešu (šEš-MEš-šu) *his brothers* **3**, 14; axe (šEš-MEš) abišu *his uncles* **3**, 15; mâre axišu (šEš-šu) *his nephews,* **3**, 15.—(W 266; HW 38[a])

axu, pl. axâti, *side* (etym. identical with axu *brother*)*:* ana a-xu agâ *on this side* **3**, 12; ana a-xi-šu-nu ullî *to their further side* (i. e. *to their rear*) **3**, 22–23.—(W 275; HW 39[b])

axâ'iš (properly *like brothers,* axâmiš, cf. šamâmiš) *together:* a-xa-iš **7**, 16.—(W 269; HW 39[b])

axâmiš (see axâ'iš) *together, mutually:* ana a-xa-meš *mutually* **1**, 22; ana tarçi a-xa-meš *opposite each other* **3**, r. 23.—(W 270; HW 39[a])

axâtu (אחות) *sister:* mâr axâtija (NIN-ia) *my nephew* **3**, r. 1; mâr axâtišu (NIN-šu) ša *the nephew of* **1**, 8.—(W 268; HW 39[a])

eṭêru, prt. eṭir(-er), prs. iṭṭir(-er), properly *to surround* (עטר), then *to hold,* or *keep, intact, to receive, buy:* ul i-ṭir-šu *he has not received it* **2**, 60; râmânšu iṭṭir *he will buy himself off* **2**, 41.—(W 325; HW 46[a]; T[c] 30)

âka (איכה) *where? whither?:* a-a-ka niškun (cohort.) *where shall we put (it)?* **17**, r. 7.—(W 338; HW 48[a])

akî (a-ki-e) *like, as:* **15**, 13; cf. kî.—(W 371; HW 52[b])

aklu *food, provisions:* I QA ak-li-šu *one* QA *of his provisions* **8**, r. 8.—(W 381; HW 54[b])

akâlu (אכל), prt. ekul, prs. ikkal, *to eat:* lîkulû (li-ku-lu) *let them feed* (of sheep) **1**, 31; ištu ... qarçeka ina pânija ekulu (i-ku-lu) *since he slandered thee* (literally, *ate thy pieces;* cf. qarçu) *before me* **6**, 10.—𝔔[t] *same,* 3 sg. e-tak-la **7**, 16; 3 pl. e-tak-lu **7**, 13.—(W 374; HW 53[a])

akâlu (properly infin. of preceding) *food:* pl. akâle (ŠA-MEŠ) **7**, 13.—(W 380; HW 54[a])

ekallu (Sumerian E-GAL *great house;* היכל) *palace:* E-GAL **2**, 63; **3**, r. 24. 25; **8**, 15. 16; **19**, l. r. 5.—(W 338; HW 48[a])

ul (cstr. of ullu *non-existence) not,* never used in prohibition like אַל; **1**, 41; **2**, 60; **4**, 26 etc.; *no!* **6**, 17.—(HW 71[b])

ilu (אל) *god:* ilu (DINGIR) **1**, 22; **8**, 15. r. 2; iluka (DINGIR-ka) *thy god* **8**, 13. Pl. ilâni (DINGIR-MEŠ) **2**, 41; **4**, 10; **18**, 20. r. l. 10; ilânija (DINGIR-MEŠ-ja) *my gods* **6**, 12; ilânika (DINGIR-MEŠ-ka) *thy gods* **14**, 24; bît ili *temple* **16**, r. l. 7.—(W 402; HW 59[b])

âlu (אהל), cstr. âl, pl. âlâni, *city:* written ER **1**, 19. 21; **3**, 12. 17; **11**, 7 etc.—(W 5; HW 59[a])

elû (עלי), prt. elî, prs. illî, *to be high, ascend.*—𝔍[t] ûtûlî (u-tu-li) *I removed* (i. e. *took up*) **14**, 20.—𝔖 ša ... ušelâ (u-še-el-la-a) *whoever offers* (to the god, העלה) **8**, r. 8.—𝔖[t] çâbe usseli'u (u-si-li-u) *I brought up soldiers* **7**, r. 10; usselûni (u-si-lu-ni) *they got* (him) *out* (up) **11**, r. 2; šumu ili ... ultelû (ul-te-lu-u) *they swore by* (made high) *the name of the god* **1**, 24.—(W 420; HW 60[b])

ullû (cf. אל, אלה) *that, yonder* (ille): axi ul-li-i *the further* (yonder) *side* **3**, 23.—(HW 73[b])

ilku *lordship, worship, reverence:* il-ku ana Ezida kunnâk *I pay heedful reverence to Ezida* **20**, 6.—(W 481; HW 70[a])

alâku (הלך), prt. illik, prs. illak, *to go, come.* Prt. sg. il-li-ku (mod. rel.) **4**, 15; pl. il-li-ku-ni **5**, 11. 12. Prs. sg. il-lak **8**, r. 1; il-la-ka **8**, 17. r. 5; pl. il-lak-u-ni **15**, r. 3. Prec. sg. lilliká-ma (lil-li-kam-ma) **1**, 34; **4**, 28.—3 fem. lû ta-li-ik **18**, r. 3; lû ta-li-ka **18**, r. 6.—1. la-al-lik **8**, 14; pl. lil-li-ku-ni **7**, r. 15; lillikûní-ma (lil-li-ku-nim-ma) **1**, 29; pl. 1. ni-il-lik-ma (cohort.) **4**, 30.—𝔔[t] *same,* sg. it-ta-lak 15, 11; i-ta-lak 16, r. 9; it-tal-ka 1, 11; 2, 10. 39.—1. at-ta-lak 7, r. 7; at-tal-ka 5, r. 10; pl. i-tal-la-ku 7, 11; it-tal-ku 1, 21; 2, 13; 15, r. 7; it-tal-ku-u-ni 7, 18; it-tal-ku-nu 19, r. 4.—Š causative. Prec. 3 pl. lu-ša-li-ku 8, r. 21.—(W 461; HW 66[b])

alpu (אלף) *ox:* pl. alpe (GUD-MEŠ) 1, 26.—(HW 75[a])

elippu (Syr. אלפא) fem. *ship:* written GIŠ-MA 18, 6. 11. r. 1.—(HW 75[a])

ultu (ul-tu).—(1) Of space, *from, away from, out of* 1, 9. 11; 2, 46; 3, 5; ultu . . . adî *from . . . to* 2, 49; 3, r. 18–19.—(2) Of time, ultu muxxi *after, since* 3, 21; 4, 11; ultu U. balṭu *as long as U. was alive* 2, 46 (cf. note *ad loc.*)—(W 411; HW 77[a])

ûmu (יום, يوم) *day* (written throughout UD + phonetic complement mu, mi): 2, 23; 3, 5; 8, 7. 10; 15, 10—Pl. ûme (UD-MEŠ) 1, 4; 2, 3; 3, 3; 14, 31.—ûmu ša *when* 2, 23; ûmi mûšu *day and night* 13, r. 6; çât ûme *the end of time* 8, r. 21. (HW 306[b])

umâ (u-ma-a) *now:* 15, r. 19; 16, r. 2; 18, r. 1.—(HW 82[b])

ammu (ammû?), pl. ammûte, fem. ammâte, *that* (ille): lippe am-mu-te *those dressings, bandages* 15, r. 8; dibbâte(?) ammete (am-me-te) *those* (such) *things(?)* 18, 16; cf. annetu, fem. pl. of annû, HW 104[a].—(HW 84[b])

umma (written um-ma but properly û-ma, i. e. demonstr. û + ma) *namely, as follows,* introducing direct discourse: 1, 23. 28. 36; 2, 14 etc.—(W 208; HW 86[a])

ummu (אם, أمّ) *mother:* ummušu (AMA-šu) *his mother* 2, 8.—(HW 85[b])

emêdu (עמד), prt. emid, prs. immid, *to stand, place.*—Ⅱ šumma idâšu ina libbi ummidûni (u-me-du-u-ni) *if he has put his hand to the matter* 14, 26; *the bandages* ummudû (u-mu-du) *are applied* 15, r. 11.—(HW 79[b])

ummânu (אָמָּן) *master workman, skilled artizan:* um-man-ka *thy master workman* 20, r. 5.—(HW 86[b])

ûmussu (ûmu) *daily:* UD-mu-us-su 4, 5. 16; 5, 4; 20, 4.—(HW 307[a])

emûqu (אמק) *force, forces, troops:* e-mu-qu 2, 16; pl. emuqešu (e-mu-ki-šu) *his forces* 2, 29; 3, r. 21.—(HW 88[b])

amâru (אמר), prt. emur, prs. immar, *to see:* ultu muxxi ša i-mu-ru-ma *after they saw* 3, 21. Prec. li-mur 12, 2.—1. lûmur (lum-mur) 6, 20.—(HW 89[b])

ammaru, cstr. ammar, *fulness, as much as:* am-mar qaqqad ubâni çixirti *the size of the tip of the little finger* 14, 22. —(HW 91ª)

immeru (אִמֵּר) *sheep:* išten immeru (LU-NITA) *a single sheep* 1, 38; pl. immereni (LU-NITA-MEŠ-ni) *our sheep* 1, 29.—(HW 91ᵇ)

amtu (אמה) *female servant, handmaid:* amtuka (GEME?-ka) *thy handmaid* 19, 2.—(HW 77ᵇ)

amâtu, cstr. amât (emû *to speak*).—(1) *word, speech:* amat šarri *the word of the king* 6, 1; a-mat-ia *my word* 2, 30.—(2) *thing* (like דבר, أمر) a-mat ša *the thing which* 2, 26; *if I learn* a-mat ša *anything which*, etc., 2, 60.—(HW 81ᵇ)

immatema (=ina matema, מתי) *if ever, in case at any time:* im-ma-tim-ma (i. e. immatéma) 4, 24.—(HW 435ᵇ)

ana, corresponds in meaning to Heb. אל and ל; written a-na or DIŠ.—(1) Of space, *to, towards:* ana ᵃˡTargibâti ittalkû *they came to T.* 1, 21; ana ᵃˡŠuxarisungur *towards S.* 2, 13. —(2) Of time, *until:* ana mâr mâre *till* (the time of our) *children's children* 6, 40.—(3) As sign of the dative, šulmu ana *greeting to* 7, 5; 9, 4; 10, 3, etc.; ana šarri . . . liqîšû *may they grant to the king* 3, 4; ana beliia likrubû *may they be gracious to my lord.*—(4) Purpose or object, ana balâṭ napšâte ša šarri uçallû *I pray for the king's life* 4, 6; ṭâbu ana alâki *it will be well to go* (literally *good for going*) 12, r. 4; ana idâtûtu *to bind the bargain* 1, 25; ana maxîri *for sale* (price) 1, 36.—(5) *respecting, in regard to:* ana mimma kalâma *in regard to everything* 20, r. 3.—(6) *in conformity with,* ana çibûtu bel šarrâni *to the king's liking* 2, 60.—For expressions like ana libbi, ana muxxi, ana pân, etc., see libbu, muxxu, pânu, etc.—(HW 94ª)

ina, corresponds in meaning to Heb. ב; written i-na or RUM.—(1) Of space, *in, at, on, into, from:* ina ᵃˡXa'âdâlu *in X.* 2, 15; ina Upî'a *at Opis* 18, r. 7; ina kussî ûšibu *seated himself on the throne* 2, 6; addan anâku qâtâ'a ina kibsâti *I shall lay my hands upon the rascals* 7, r. 8; ina bît Nabû errab *he shall go into the temple of N.* 8, r. 9; ina kutallišunu *from their side* 2, 20.—(2) Of time, *in, during:* ina timâli *yesterday* 14, 15; 15, r. 5.—ina arax Šabâṭi *in the month of Shebat* 8, r. 16; ina pânâtu *beforehand* 7, 20.—(3) State or condition, ina puluxti *in a state of panic* 2, 16; ina qašti ramîti *with bow unstrung* 2, 42.—(4) Manner, ina lâ mûdânûti *in an unscientific manner* 15, r. 8.—(5) Means, ina bûbâta tadûkâ *ye have slain with famine* 2, 55.—For expressions like ina libbi, ina muxxi, ina pân, etc., cf. libbu, muxxu, pânu, etc.—(HW 95ª)

înu (עַיִן, عين) *eye:* uzu (i. e. šîru)-ši 1, 35; pl. înûšu (ši²-šu) *his eyes* 8, 11; cf. birtu.—(W 348; HW 49ª)

enna (כְּעַן, עַתָּה) *now:* adî ša en-na *until now* 5, r. 13.—(HW 103ᵇ)

annû, fem. annîtu, pl. annûti, fem. annâti, *this* (hic): fem. an-ni-tu 4, 36, pl. an-nu-te 7, r. 17.—(HW 103ᵇ)

ennâ (הִנֵּה) *lo! behold!:* en-na 1, 33; 2, 31. 51. 56; 4, 21; 5, r. 7.—(HW 103ᵇ)

anâku (אָנֹכִי) *I:* a-na-ku 2, 35; 6, 7. 32; 7, r. 8; 8, 13; 16, 13; ana(diš)-ku 2, 35; 6, 23; 13, r. 6.—(HW 101ª)

annaka *here:* an-na-ka 19, r. 3; a-na-ka 7, r. 12.—(Cf. PSBA. xvii. 237)

anînu, anîni (אֲנַחְנוּ), **nîni** (نحن) *we:* a-ni-ni 3, r. 4; ni-i-ni(?) 18, 15.—(HW 103ª)

unqu, pl. unqâte, *ring, signet:* un-qu 2, 32.—(HW 104ᵇ)

annûšiᵐ *just now, immediately, forthwith:* an-nu-šiᵐ 16, 7; 19, r. 3. 9.—(HW 104ª)

âsû (properly *helper*, prt. of asû *to support;* Syr. אָסיָא) *physician:* pl. âse (a-zu-meš) 16, 5.—(HW 107ª).

issi (by-form of itti with spiration of ת, cf. §43, APR. 107, n. 2) *with:* i-si-ia *with me* 7, r. 15; is-si-ka *with thee* 9, r. 8; is-si-šu-nu 19, r. 9; i-si-šu-nu 7, 8. 11. 15; 16, 12, *with them.*—(HW 110ª)

asâte *reins* (pl. of a noun asû): mukîl asâte (su-pa-meš) *the charioteer* 8, 21.—(HW 107ᵇ)

appu (אַף), pl. appê, *nose, face:* ap-pi 14, 13; 15, r. 2. 10.—(HW 104ª)

aplu, cstr. apil, pl. aple, *son:* Ummanigaš apil (a) Amedirra *U. son of A.* 3, r. 16; apil(a)-šu ša *the son of* 5, 7; apil šipri (a-kin) *messenger* 1, 17. 33.—(HW 113ª)

epêšu, prt. epuš, prs. ippuš, ippaš.—(1) Transitive, *to do, make, perform.* Prt. 1 pl. nîpušûni (ni-pu-šu-u-ni) 15, 9. Prs. niqû ip-pa-aš *will offer* (make) *a sacrifice* 8, r. 7; dullu ippušû *are doing duty* 7, r. 21; ša tepušâ (te-pu-ša-') *which ye have done* 6, 35. 36. Prec. parçe ša ilâni . . . lîpušû *may they perform the commands of the gods* 8, r. 13.—(2) Intransitive, *to do, act, be active;* kî ša ilá'u li-pu-uš *let him act as he pleases* 4, 35; nindema ilâni . . . ip-pu-šu-ma *if the gods will bestir themselves* 2, 42.—$\mathfrak{Q}^t$ *same,* sîxu etépuš (i-te-pu-uš) *he made a revolt* 3, r. 18; mimma . . . bîšu etepšû (i-te-ip-šu) *they practiced all that was evil* 5, 14.—$\mathfrak{N}$ Passive, niqû in-ni-pa-aš *a sacrifice will be offered* 8, 19.—$\mathfrak{J}$ *to carry on:* elippu . . . nîburu tuppaš (tu-pa-aš) *the ship . . . is carrying on a ferry* 18, 13; lû tuppiš (tu-pi-iš) *let it carry on* 18, r. 5; uppušû (u-pu-šu) *they are carrying on* 18, r. 14.—(HW 117^a)

açû (אצי, وضو), prt. ûçî, prs. uççâ, *to go out, forth.* Prt. 1 sg. ûçâ (u-ça-') 3, 6; pl. ûçû (u-çu-u) 5, 9; ûçûni (u-çu-u-ni) 15, r. 13. Prs. uççâ (uç-ça) 8, 16.—$\mathfrak{Q}^t$ *same,* pl. ittáçû (i-ta-çu) 7, r. 2; $\mathfrak{N}^t$ ittûçûni (it-tu-çu-u-ni) 7, 17.—$\mathfrak{S}$ Causative, Prs. ušeçâ (u-še-ça-a) 8, r. 2; pl. ušeçûni (u-še-çu-u-ni) 7, r. 18.—(HW 237^a)

âru (אִיָּר) *Iyyar,* the second month of the Babylonian calendar: arax âru (ITI-GUD) 8, 7.—(HW 34^b)

urû (אֻרְוֹת) *stable:* u-ru-u ša ilâni *the stable of the gods* (i. e. the stable for horses used in religious processions, etc.) 8, 20. (HW 130^a)

erêbu (ערב, غرب), prt. erub, prs. irrub, irrab, *to enter:* ûmuša . . . irubu (i-ru-bu) *the day he entered* 2, 24; irrab (ir-rab) *he will enter* 8, 9; irrab (e-rab) *he may enter* 8, r. 9; lîrubû (li-ru-bu) *let them go in* 16, 11.—$\mathfrak{Q}^t$ ina libbi âli e-tar-ba *he came into the city* 11, 8.—$\mathfrak{S}$ Causative, ilu ušeçâ u ussaxxar u-še-rab *he will take the god forth and bring him in again* 8, r. 4; adû . . . lâ ušerabanâšina (u-še-ra-ba-na-ši-na) *before we are brought in* (literally *one brings us in*) 19, r. 7.—$\mathfrak{S}^t$ puluxti ulteribû (ul-te-ri-bu) *they have been invaded by* (literally *caused to enter*) *panic* 2, 18.—(HW 126^b)

ardu (written NITA), pl. ardâni (written NITA-MEŠ, NITA-MEŠ-ni) *servant, slave:* ardû'a *my servant* 6, 14; ardúka *thy servant* 1, 2; 2, 1; 3, 1; 18, 2, etc.; ardâni *servants* 3, 6. r. 3; 19, 8; ardânika *thy servants* 12, 2; 17, 2.—(HW 129^a)

arâdu (ירד for ורד), prt. ûrid, prs. urrad, *to go down, descend.*—$\mathfrak{S}^t$ Causative, kaspu ina libbi ussérida (u-si-ri-da) *wherein he conveyed the money down* (the river) 18, 8; çâbe usseridûni (u-si-ri-du-ni) akâle *the soldiers took provisions down* (with them) 7, 12.—(HW 240^b)

arxu (ירח, Eth. *warx*), cstr. arax, *month:* arxu, arax (ITI) 8, 7. r. 16; 11, 6; 17, 13, etc.—(HW 241b)

araxsamna (i. e. *eighth month*) *Marcheshvan*, the eighth month of the Babylonian calendar: [arax]APIN 5, 17. r. 11. 22.—(HW 242a)

arku, fem. ariktu, *long* (arâku)': ûme arkûti (ar-ku-ti 17, 8; GID-DA-MEŠ 19, 6) *a long life* (literally *long days*).—(HW 133b).

arâku (ארך), prt. erik, *to be, or become, long.*—Infin. a-ra-ku *prolongation* 1, 4; 2, 3; 3, 3.—(HW 133a)

arkâniš (from arku *rear;* ירך, ورك) *afterwards, later:* ar-ka-niš 5, 14.—(HW 243a).

eršu (עֶרֶשׂ) *bed, couch:* eršu (GIŠ-NA) ša Nabû *the couch of N.* 8, 8; bît erši (E-GIŠ-NA) *bed-chamber* 8, 9.—(HW 141a)

ašâbu (ישב for ושב), prt. ûšib, prs. uššab, *to sit, dwell:* ša . . . ina kussî u-ši-i-bu (pause form) *who seated himself upon the throne* 2, 6; nu-uš-šab *we will dwell* 2, 15; partic. âšib (a-šib) *inhabitants* (collective) 4, 25.—$\mathfrak{N}^t$ *same,* it-tu-šib (i. e. ittûšib = intaušib) 15, 13.—$\mathfrak{S}^t$ Causative, šubtu ussešibu (u-si-ši-bu) *he had laid an ambush* 7, 21.—(HW 244a)

išdu (אשד, אשדה) *foundation:* iš-du ša bît abiia *the prop and stay of my father's house* 6, 15.—(HW 142b)

ištu, written TA.—(1) Of space, *from:* ištu Deri issapra *he sends word from Der* 16, 18; ištu pâni dâme ûçûni *the blood flows forth in spite of* (literally *from before*) the bandages 15, r. 12.—(2) Of time, *since:* ištu Šamaš libbašu issuxa *since S. perverted his understanding* 6, 8.—(HW 152a)

aššatu (אִשָּׁה, انثى) *woman, wife:* aššatsu (DAM-šu) *his wife* 2, 8.—(HW 106a)

išten (עַשְׁתֵּי) *one, a single, a certain* (quispiam): written I-en; išten muššarû *one inscription* 16, r. 3; išten immeru *a single sheep* 1, 38; išten qallu *a certain servant* 5, r. 7.—(HW 153a)

atâ (properly impv. of atû *to see*) *well, now, see!:* [umâ a-ta]-a *now, see now!* 18, r. 1.—(HW 156b)

atta (אַתָּה, انت) *thou:* at-ta 6, 33.—(HW 160a)

itti (properly genit. of ittu *side,* fem. of idu *hand*) *with:* it-ti 2, 19; 3, 25; it-ti-šu-nu *with them* 2, 25; it-ti U.

ušazgûšu *they withhold it from U.* (like מְאַת) 2, 58.—(HW 154^{b}).—Compare issi.

itu'u, an official title: ^{amel}itu-'-u 7, r. 11; ^{amel}Šanû i-tu-' K. 1359, Col. II, 11 (PSBA, May, '89).—(HW 157^{a})

etêqu (עתק), prt. etiq, prs. ittiq, *to pass.* Inf. e-te-qa *route* (of procession) 8, r. 5.—(HW 159^{a})

atâru (יתר = ותר) *to exceed, surpass.*—Ⅲ causative, *to increase:* ut-tir remu aškunáka *I have granted thee greater favor* (than ever) 6, 24.—(HW 248^{a}).

ב

bâ'u (בוא), prt. and prs. ibâ, *to come:* apil šipri ibâšu (i-ba-aš-šu) *a messenger has come to him* 1, 17.—(HW 167^{b})

bâbu (Aram. בָּבָא, باب, reduplicated form from בוא) *gate; part, portion:* bâbšu (KA-šu) *his portion* 2, 47; cf. T^{c} 56^{b}.—(HW 165^{b})

bûbâtu *famine, hunger:* bu-ba-a-ta 2, 55.—plur. of

bûbûtu (properly *emptiness:* reduplicated form from בהו) *famine, hunger:* bu-bu-u-ti 6, 27.—(HW 166^{a})

bâdu (cf. بادت الشمس) *sunset, evening*(?)*:* ina timâli kî ba-di *yesterday evening* 14, 16; 15, r. 5.—Cf. the following, from Harper's Letters: ûmu VI ana ba-a-di egirtušu annîtu ina muxxiia issapra *he sent me this letter the evening of the 6th* (of the month) H. 101, 11; ina ši'âri ša ba-a-di ri-in-ku ina ^{âl}Tarbiçi *to-morrow evening there will be a libation in T.* H. 47, 7; ina ši'ari ûmu IV ana ba-a-di Nabû Tašmetu^{m} ina bît erši irrubû *to-morrow, the 4th, at sunset, Nabû and Tašmet will enter the bed-chamber* H. 366, 6; sîse ana ba-a-di lušaqbî sîse lušaçbitu *I will stable the horses this evening and assign them quarters* (for lušaqbî, cf. qabû *stable, pen,* HW 578^{b}; for šuçbutu *to station, place,* cf. HW 562^{a}). Cf. Hebraica, x. 196; AJSL., xiv. 16.

bîd (synonym of kî) *as, like:* bi-id šarru išápar *as the king commands* (sends) 16, 16; ultu bîd ana Elamti . . . ûçû *since they went away to Elam* 5, 8; ultu bîd . . . nušebila *since we sent* 5, r. 11.—(HW 190^{a})

belu (בעל) *lord:* belú'a (EN-a) 4, 7. 21; beliia (EN-ia) 4, 7. 33, (be-ili-ia) 1, 1. 6, belî (be-ili) *my lord;* belika (EN-ka) 6, 28, (EN-ka-a) 6, 18 *thy lord;* belišu (EN-šu) 6, 31 *his lord;* beluni (EN-ni) 12, 11. r. 2, belini (EN-ni) 12,

l. 6. 8 (EN-i-ni) 17, 6. 11. r. 3, *our lord;* bel (EN) šarrâni *the lord of kings* 1, l. 5.—(HW 163[a])

balû *to worship, be submissive:* immatema . . . ul ibalû (i-ba-lu) *if they will not submit* 4, 26.—(HW 173[b])

balâṭu (מלט, פלט properly *survive;* cf. חיה), prt. ibluṭ, prs. ibáluṭ, once ibálaṭ, *to live; to recover from illness:* ibálaṭ (i-ba-laṭ) *he will recover* 14, 31; balṭu (bal-ṭu) *he was alive* 2, 46; ina libbi balṭû (bal-ṭu) *they live (subsist) upon it* 2, 45.—𝕴 ul u-bal-laṭ-ka *I will not let thee live* 1, 41; ana bulluṭ (bu-luṭ) napšâte *for the preservation of the life of* 8, r. 11.—(HW 174[b])

balâṭu (properly infin. of preceding) *life:* [ba-laṭ] napišti 13, r. l. 2; balâṭ (TIN) napšâte *life, preservation* 4, 6; 5, 6; 20, 5; lale balâṭi (TIN) *fullness, enjoyment, of life* 10, 10.—(HW 175[a])

beltu (fem. of belu), pl. belêti, *lady:* belit (NIN) Kidimuri *the lady of K.* 10, 6.—(HW 163[b])

banû (בני), prt. ibnî, prs. ibánî, *to make, build, beget:* bânû (properly participle) *ancestor;* mâre bânûti (DU-KAK-MEŠ) *free-born citizens, nobles* (properly *sons of ancestors*) 3, 16.—(HW 178[b])

banû *bright, honorable, excellent:* ban (ba-an) ša tepušâ *the excellent (service) that ye have done* (cstr. before ša) 6, 36; ša ina pâniịa banû (ban-u) *which is honorable in my sight* 6, 39.—(HW 180[a])

BAR a measure of some kind, 2, 56.

bûru (באר, בור) *well, cistern:* ina bûri (PÚ) ittuqut *he fell into a well* 11, r. 1.—(HW 164[b])

barû, prt. ibrî, prs. ibárî, *to see.*—𝕴 Causative, lâ ubarrî (u-bar-ri) *I have not disclosed* 16, 14.—(HW 182[a])

bîrtu (barû) *glance, sight:* bîrit îni *clear, plain sight;* ina bîrit (bi-rit) îni lumandid *let him make it clearly understood* (literally *measure out in plain view*) 1, 34.—(HW 183[a])

bîrtu (בִּירָה) *fortress, castle:* šulmu ana [al]bîrât (bi-rat) *greeting to the fortresses* 7, 5; bir-ti-šu *the* (literally *his*) *fortress* (ZA. ii. 321) 7, r. 10.—(HW 185[a])

bîšu (באשׁ) *bad, evil:* bi-i-šu 5, 13; dibbeka bîšûtu (bi-šu-u-tu) *evil words about thee* (cf. דִּבָּתָם רָעָה, Gen. xxxvii. 2) 6, 6.—(HW 165[a])

bašû (properly ba+šu *in him;* cf. Eth. *bô, bôtû*), prt. ibšî, prs. ibášî, *to be, exist.*—Prs. sg. i-ba-aš-ši 14, 22; i-ba-aš-šu-u-ni (mod. rel.) **8**, r. 7; pl. i-ba-aš-šu-u **2**, 12; **3**, r. 5; ibaši'u (i-ba-ši-u) **15**, r. 9.—(HW 188ᵃ)

bîtu (בית), pl. bîtâte, written E, E-MEŠ, *house;* with reference to gods, *temple:* bît Marduk-erba *the house of M-e.* **19**, r. 6; ina bîti *in the house of* **9**, r. 4; rab-bîti *majordomo* **2**, 52; bît ili *temple* **16**, r. 1. 7; ilu mâr bîti *the god of the temple* **20**, 10; bît Nabû *the temple of N.* **8**, 12. r. 9; bitâte karâni *store-houses for wine* **17**, r. 1.—(HW 171ᵇ)

bitxallu *riding horse:* pl. bitxallâti, [amel] ša bit-xal-la-ti *the cavalry* **7**, r. 22; cf. Hebraica, x. 109, 198.—(HW 190ᵇ)

ג

gabbu (usually in genit. gabbi) *totality, all, every:* generally placed after, and in apposition to, the word qualified; maççarâte gab-bu *all the guards* **10**, r. 6; qinnašu gab-bi *his whole family* **2**, 8; mâtsunu gab-bi *their whole country;* bel ṭâbâtešu gab-bi *all his partizans* **2**, 24; šarnuppi gab-bi *every šarnuppu* **2**, 51; agâ gab-bi *all these parts, this country* (literally *all this*) **2**, 16.—(HW 192ᵃ)

gamâru (גמר), prt. igmur, prs. igámar, *to complete, to pay:* tapšuru igámar-ma (i-gam-mar-ma) *he will pay a ransom* **2**, 40.—(HW 199ᵇ)

gušûru (gašâru *to make strong*) *beam, timber:* pl. gušûre (GIŠ-GUŠUR-MEŠ) annûte *this timber* (literally *these beams*) **7**, r. 17.—(HW 207ᵃ)

ד

de'u (دوي) *disease, plague:* kîma de'i (di-e) xurrurû *they are ravaged as though (by) a plague* **2**, 17.—(HW 297ᵃ)

dibbu (דִּבָּה), pl. dibbe, *word, speech:* dibbušu (dib-bu-šu) *his word* **20**, r. 4; pl. dib-be (dib-bi) agâ *these words* **5**, r. 15; dibbe ka'âmânûtu *reliable words* **1**, 41; dibbeka (dib-bi-ka) bîšûtu *evil words about thee* (cf. bîšu) **6**, 5; dibbâte (?) ammete (?) (dib?-ba-te am-me-te?) *these things, such matters*(?) (cf. דבר, أمر, *thing*) **18**, 16.—(HW 209ᵇ)

dabâbu, prt. idbub, prs. idábub, *to speak, converse:* issišunu lidbubu (lid-bu-bu) *let him converse with them* **16**, 12.—Qᵗ *same,* iddébub (id-di-bu-ub) **2**, 25; cf. dînu.—(HW 208ᵇ)

dâku, prt. idûk, prs. idâk, *to kill:* šuxdû-ma . . . lâ a-du-ku *not willingly would I have slain* 6, 16; tadûkâ (ta-du-ka) *ye have slain* 2, 23; idûkû (i-du-ku) *they slew* II, r. 3; dûkâ (du-u-ka) *slay ye!* 3, 10.—Infin. dâku, ana muxxi dâkika (GAZ-ka) ilmû *they have planned thy destruction* 6, 22; ana dâki (GAZ) iddinûka *they have given thee over to death* 6, 11; ina pâni da-a-ku ša axiia *in order to slay my brother* 4, 15.—Q[t] *same*, iddûkû (id-du-ku) *they slew* 3, 17; taddûkâ (ta-ad-du-ka) *ye have slain* 2, 56.—(HW 212[a])

dîktu *slaughter, slaying:* di-ik-ti dûkâ *slay ye!* 3, 10.—(HW 212[b])

dîkîtu (*Nisbeh* form) *troop of soldiers*(?)*:* ina qât di-ki-tu *accompanied by a troop* 2, 38.

dullu (dalâlu *to serve*; דלל *to be poor, dependent*) *work, duty, service:* dul-lu 6, 33; 7, r. 21; 15, 8.—(HW 219[b])

dalâpu (دلف) *to go:* adálap (a-dal-lap) *I will go* 4, 22. —(HW 217[b] below)

dâmu (דם) *blood:* pl. dâme (UŠ-MEŠ) 15, r. 2. 6. 13. 17.—(HW 220[a])

dînu (דין) *judgment, cause:* di-i-ni ittišunu iddébub *he upbraided them* (literally *plead a cause with them*) 2, 25.—(HW 215[b])

duppu (Syr. דַּפָּא) *tablet, letter:* duppu (IM) Bel-upâq *letter of B.-u.* 20, 1.—(HW 226[a])

dupšarru (Sumerian DUB *tablet* + SAR *to write*) *scribe, secretary:* dupšar (A-BA) mâti *the secretary of state* 9, 1; dupšar (A-BA) ekalli *the secretary of the palace* 19, 1. r. 5.—(HW 227[b])—Cf. note on 9, 1, p. 47.

deqû, prt. idqî, prs. idaqî, *to gather, collect:* qaštašunu . . . idqû (id-ku-u) *they assembled their forces* 3, r. 5; ebûru deqî (di-e-qi) *the harvest is gathered* 16, r. 10.—(HW 216[a], sub דכא)

dârû (*Nisbeh* of dâru, דור *to endure*), *enduring, everlasting:* šanâte dârâte *never ending years* 17, 9.—(HW 213[a])

ז

zagû, perhaps *to stand.*—Š ušazgûšu (u-ša-az-gu-u-šu) *they withhold it* (i. e. cause to stop) 2, 59; dînâtu attû'a . . . u-ša-az-gu-u *I have established* (i. e. caused to stand firm) *my rights*, Behistun (III R. 39) 9.—(HW 260[a], sub זקה)

zilliru (zi-il-li-ru) an Elamite official title **2**, 11.—(HW 256[b])

zîmu (זִיו Dan. ii. 31, v. 6; properly, *brightness*) *face, form, appearance:* żîmišu (zi-me-šu) malû *his complete health* (literally *full form*) **1**, 14.—(HW 252[b])

zunnu *rain;* written A-AN-MEŠ **16**, r. 8, where the plural sign (MEŠ) has merely a collective force.—(HW 259[b])

ח (خ)

xi'lânu, xiialânu *troops:* xi-'-la-a-nu **4**, 8; xi-ia-la-ni-ia *my troops* **3**, 22.—(HW 275[a])

xubtu *booty, prisoners* (cf. xabâtu): xubte (xu-ub-ti) CL ixtabtûni *they captured 150 prisoners* **3**, 18–19.—(HW 269[a])

xabâtu, prt. ixbut, *to plunder, take prisoner:* impv. plur. xubtu xubtânu (xu-ub-ta-a-nu) *take prisoners!* (=xubtâni) **3**, 11.—Q[t] ixtabtûni (ix-tab-tu-ni) *they captured* **3**, 19.—(HW 268[b])

xadû (חֶדְוָה *pleasure*), prt. ixdû, ixdî, *to rejoice, be glad.* Stem of šuxdû q. v.

xazânu (חַזָּן) *prefect, superior:* xa-za-nu ša bît Nabû *the prefect of the temple of N.* **8**, 12.—(HW 272[a])

xakâmu, prs. ixákim, *to understand.*—Š lušaxkim (lu-šax-ki-im) *I will give directions, explain* **15**, r. 19.—(HW 276[a])

xalqu *fugitive, deserter:* pl. xalqûte (XA-A-MEŠ) **7**, 9; xal-qu H. **245**, 11; xal-qu-te H. **245**, 5. r. 11.

xalâqu (Eth. *xalqa*), prt. ixliq, prs. ixáliq, *to flee:* kî ix-li-qu *when he fled* **1**, 10; ša ix-li-qa *who fled* **2**, 5; adî lâ axáliqa (a-xal-li-qa) *before I fled* **2**, 26.—(HW 279[b])

xamaṭṭa (xamadda) *help, aid:* xa-maṭ-ṭa **8**, r. 17.—(HW 281[a], sub xamât)

xannû, xanni'u (=annû) *this:* lakû sikru xa-ni-u *this poor fellow* **14**, 10.—The following additional examples are taken from Harper's Letters: xa-an-ni-i H. **19**, r. 12; H. **306**, 10; H. **357**, r. 10; xa-an-ni-e H. **355**, 15; xa-ni-e H. **311**, 13; xa-an-ni-ma H. **358**, 29. r. 17; xa-an-nim-ma H. **362**, r. 1.—Pl. xa-nu-u-te H. **121**, 8; xa-nu-te H. **99**, 6; H. **121**, r. 10; xa-an-nu-ti H. **306**, 5. r. 7.—(HW 284[a])

xasâsu, prt. ixsus, prs. ixásas, *to think, perceive, understand: if the king* lâ xassu (xa-as-su) *does not understand* **5**, r. 24.—Q[t] kî amât . . . ax-tas-su *when I learn anything* **2**,

61.—𝔍 xussu (xu-us-su) *he is well informed* 20, r. 6.—For these syncopated forms cf. § 97.—(HW 284[b])

xepû, prt. ixpî, prs. ixápî, *to destroy:* ultu muxxi . . . bît abiia ixpû (ix-pu-u) *since he destroyed my father's house* 4, 14.—(HW 286[a])

xarâdu, prs. ixárid.—𝔔[t] ix-te-ri-di 15, 11.—(HW 289[a])

xarâçu (חרץ) properly *to cut,* then *to decide, fix, establish:* xarâçu (xa-ra-çu) ša dibbe agâ *confirmation of these words* 5, r. 14; ṭenšunu xariç (xa-ri-iç) *he has accurate news of them* 3, r. 25.—(HW 292[a], sub xarîçu)

xarâru, prs. ixárar, *to plow.*—𝔍 xurrurû (xur-ru-ru) *they are ravaged* (literally *plowed up*).—(HW 292[a])

ט

ṭa'âbu (d, p? طبع?), prt. iṭ'ib, *to oppress* (?).—𝔍 naxnaxûtu u-ṭa-u-bu *they oppress, interfere with, the breathing* 15, r. 12.—(HW 722[a], sub (ף?)דאב)

ṭâbu (طاب, يطيب), prt. iṭîb, prs. iṭâb, *to be good, well:* ṭa-a-ba ana alâki *the conditions are favorable for the journey* (literally, *it is good for going*) 12, r. 3. 4. 5. 7; libbaka . . . lû-ṭa-a-ba *may thy heart be of good cheer* 9, r. 3; lû-ṭa-ab-ka 6, 3; libbu ša šarri . . . lû ṭa-a-ba 14, 30; lû DUG-GA 16, r. 12; libbu ša mûr šârri . . . lâ ṭâbšu (DUG-GA-šu) 10, r. 8.—(HW 290[b])

ṭûbu (טוב) *good, welfare:* ṭûb(i) libbi u ṭûb (i) šîri(e) *health of mind and body* (ṭu-ub) 1, 4. 5; 10, 8. 9; 19, 6. 7; (DUG-ub) 14, 6; 15, 5. 6; (ṭu-bi) 2, 2; 3, 2. 3.—(HW 300[b] reads ṭub and explains as cstr. of ṭubbu infin. 𝔍 of ṭâbu)

ṭâbtu, pl. ṭâbâte, *benefit, kindness:* ṭâbâte (MUN-XI-A) *favors* 6, 39; bel ṭâbâte (EN MUN-XI-A-MEŠ) *partizans, friends* 2, 12. 24. 47.—(HW 301[a])

ṭebêtu, *Tebeth,* the tenth month of the Babylonian calendar; written ITI-AB 17, 13.—(HW 298[b])

ṭemu (טעם) *news, information:* ṭe-e-mu 1, 24; 2, 4; 3, r. 15; ṭenšunu (ṭe-en-šu-nu) *news about them* 3, r. 24.—(HW 297[a]; cf. Guthe's Ezra-Nehemiah, p. 35)

י

iânu (אין) *not:* iânû (ia-'-nu-u, i. e. iânu + interrog. enclitic *u*) *is it not so?* 6, 25.—(HW 49[a])

i̯âši *me:* šulmu i̯a-a-ši *it is well with* (as to) *me* 6, 2.—(HW 51[b])

i̯âtu *mine:* elippu šî i̯a-a-tu *that ship of mine* 18, 6; i̯a-a-tu lû tallika *let mine* (i. e. my ship) *go* 18, r. 6.

כ

KU (?) 1, 26.

kî (כְּ, כִּי), written ki-i, ki.—(1) Preposition, *as, like, according to:* kî adî *according to compact* 1, 23.—(2) Conjunction; (a) *when,* kî... ittalka *when he arrives* 2, 38; kî içbatu *when he received* 2, 47; kî itbû *when they reached* 3, 13; kî iplaxû *having become afraid* 3, 24; kî upaxxir *having assembled* 2, 24; cf. also 1, 9. 12; 2, 7. 9. 51. 54; 5, 12. 15. 19; 20, 12;—(b) *if,* kî... taltapra *if thou sendest* 1, 36; kî... çibû *if he wishes* 5, r. 14; kî... maxru *if it be agreeable* 2, 31; 4, 26; kî... axtassu *if I learn* 2, 60; kî ša... lâ xassu *if he does not understand* 5, r. 21–24;—(c) *that,* îdû kî *they know that* 4, 11;—(d) *as, since,* kî... karmatûni *since it is bottled;*—(e) *although,* kî uše'iduš *although he has applied for it* 2, 59.—(3) Adverb, kî ša šaṭrâ *just as they* (the letters) *were written* 5, r. 20; kî... kî *now... again* (literally *thus... thus,* introducing direct discourse; cf. note ad loc.) 2, 14–15.—(HW 325[b])

ka'âmânu (1) Adjective, *steadfast, reliable:* pl. dibbe ka'âmânûtu (ka-a-a-ma-nu-tu) *reliable words* 1, 41.—(2) Adverb, libbaka ka-a-a-ma-ni· lû ṭâba *may thy heart ever be of good cheer* 9, r. 2.—(HW 321[b])

kibistu (kabâsu, כבס; properly, *trampling,* what is trampled under foot; cf. sikiptu) *base fellow, rascal:* addan anâku qâtâ'a ina kibsâte (kib-sa-ti) *I will lay my hands upon the rascals* 7, r. 8.

kâdu *military post, garrison*(?)*:* ka-a-du 3, 8. r. 2. 12.—(HW 725[a])

kâlu (כול), prt. ikûl, *to hold, bear.*—𝕴 part. mukîl (mu-kil) asâte *charioteer* (literally *holder of the reins*) 8, 21.—𝕴[t] uktîl (uk-ti-il) 15, 12.—(HW 319[b])

kalû (כלא), prt. iklû, iklâ, prs. ikálû, *to check, restrain.*—𝕹 dâme ikkali'u (ik-ka-li-u) *the hemorrhage will be checked* 15, r. 17.—(HW 328[a])

kalbu (כלב) *dog:* kal-bi 2, 62.—(HW 328[b])

kilâle (כִּלְאַיִם, Eth. *kĕl'ē*) *both:* rabe-qiçiri̯a kilâle (ki-la-le) *both my chiefs of battalion* 7, r. 4.—(HW 331[b])

kalâmu (= kâlu + ma) *totality, all:* ana mimma kalâmu (ka-la-mu) *in regard to anything whatever* **20**, r. 3.—(HW 329[a])

kalâmu *to see.*—**Ⅱ** *to show* lukallimûnâši (lu-kal-li-mu-na-ši) *let them show us* **17**, r. 4.—(HW 332[b])

kîma (= kî + emphatic ma, Heb. כְּמוֹ) *like, as:* ki-ma de'i *as (with) a plague* **2**, 17.—(HW 326[a])

kamâsu, prt. ikmis, prs. ikámis (properly *to bow, fall down*), *to settle, dwell, in a place; to remove* (i. e., settle elsewhere): kî ikmisû (ik-me-su) *when they had removed, left* **2**, 9. The following examples are taken from Harper's Letters: issuri ina bîtika-ma kam-mu-sa-ka, *if indeed thou art dwelling at home* H. **97**, 7–8; ilâni ammar ina Esaggil kam-mu-su-ni *all the gods that dwell in Esaggil* H. **119**, 7–8; ilâni ammar ina bîti kam-mu-su-ni *all the gods that dwell in the temple* H. **120**, 7–8; ištu âl bît abika bîd atta kam-mu-sa-ka-ni *when you removed from the city of your father's house* H. **46**, 11.—(HW 336[a])

kanû, **Ⅱ** *to care for, give heed to:* ilku ana Ezida kunnâk (kun-na-ak) *I pay heedful reverence to E.* **20**, 9.—(HW 337[b])

kanâku, prt. iknuk, *to seal, execute a contract:* [amel]rešu iknukûni (ik-nu-ku-u-ni) *the officer who executed the contract* **19**, r. 8.—(HW 589[a], sub קנך)

kunukku *seal, sealed document:* kunukku (TAK-ŠID) ina qâtišunu *provided with a warrant* **7**, 8.—(HW 589[b])

kenûtu (כון) *loyalty:* kenûtka (ki-nu-ut-ka) *thy loyalty* **6**, 23.—(HW 322[a])

kussû (כִּסֵּא) *throne:* kussî (GIŠ-GU-ZA) **2**, 6.—(HW 343[a])

KAS-BU (or **KAS-GID?**) *double hour:* II KAS-BU qaqqar *two double hours of ground* **3**, 12.

kis(i)limu *Chisleu*, the ninth month of the Babylonian calendar: ITI-GAN **II**, 6.—(HW 344[a])

kaspu (כסף) *silver, money:* kas-pu **15**, 10; **18**, 7; ana kas-pi (AZAG-UD) *for money* **1**, 27.—(HW 345[a])

kasâru, prt. iksir, prs. ikásir, *to dam, check, confine.*—**Ⅳ** šâru ikkasir (i-ka-si-ir) *the air will be kept away* **15**, r. 16. —(HW 345[b])

kissûtu (= kissatu; Aram. כִּסָּא, כִּסְּתָא) *fodder* (for cattle, etc.): [še]ki-su-tu **18**, 15. r. 8; [še]ki-is-su-tu ana [immer]U-SI-MEŠ H. **306**, r. 12.

kûru (for kur'u; Syr. אֶתְכְּרֵהּ *to fall ill*) *distress, trouble:* ša kûri (ku-ri) înâšu *his eyes are diseased* (ša like ذو; cf. BA. i. 384 below) 14, 11.—(HW 352b)

kirû *grove:* kirû (GIŠ-SAR) ša Ašur *the* (sacred) *grove of Ašur* 11, 9; k. ša Nabû *of Nabû* 8, 7.—(HW 353a)

karâbu, prt. ikrub, prs. ikárab, *to be gracious to, bless:* ana šarri likrubû (lik-ru-bu) *may they bless, be gracious to, the king* 4, 4; 5, 4; 11, 5; 12, 9; 13, 8; 18, 5; 19, 6; lik-ru-bu-šu *may they bless him* 12, 15.—(HW 350a)

karâbu; ul kir-bi-ku-ma (1 sing. permans. like çixriku?) 2, 61; cf. ul kir-bi-ka H. 202, 7.

karâmu *to bottle:* 3 fem. permans. kar-ma-tu-u-ni *is bottled* 17, 14; cf. note ad loc.

kurummatu *provisions, food:* pl. kurummâtani (ŠUK-XI-A-a-ni) 2, 54. 57; kurummâtíni (ŠUK-XI-A-i-ni) 2, 53 *our provisions.*—(HW 354b)

karânu *wine:* written GIŠ-GEŠ-TIN 17, r. 6; bîtâte karâni (E-GEŠ-TIN-MEŠ) *store-houses for wine* 17, r. 1.—(HW 354b)

karâru (modern Arabic كرّز *to purify*) *to sanctify, consecrate: the city of Calah* eršu ša Nabû tak-kar-ra-ar *will consecrate the couch of Nabû.*—Cf. the liturgical text K. 164 (BA. ii. 635), ll. 15. 32. 47.

kettu (properly feminine of kenu; כון) *truth:* ki-e-tu 16, 13.—(HW 323a)

kutallu (כֹּתֶל, Cant. ii. 19; Aram. כתל, Dan. v. 5; כֻּתְלַיָּא, Ezr. v. 8, *wall*) *side:* ina ku-tal-li-šu-nu *from their side* 2, 20.—(HW 362a)

ל

lâ (לא) *not:* 2, 26. 29. 65; 4, 16; 16, 14. 15; 19, r. 7, etc.—(HW 363a)

lû (ל, ل; cf. Haupt in JHU. Circ., xiii., No. 114, 107, July '94). (1) Asseverative particle, *verily, indeed:* lû îdû *verily they know* 4, 11.—(2) Precative particle, lû šulmu ana *greeting to* 7, 3; 8, 3; 10, 3, etc.; lû tallik *let it* (the ship) *come* 17, r. 3; šarru lû îdî *may the king know* 5, r. 27; libbaka lû ṭâbka *may thy heart be of good cheer* 6, 3.—(HW 373b)

la'û (لوى), prs. ilâ'î, ilé'î: kî ša i-la-'u *as he pleases* 4, 34; kî ša a-li-'-u-' *as I please* H. 402, r. 5.—(HW 364b)

libbu (לב, לבב), written lib-bu (bi, ba), ša, ša-bi(ba, bu).—(1) *heart, mind:* libbaka lû ṭâbka *may thy heart be of good cheer* **6**, 3 (cf. ṭâbu, ṭûb libbi ṭûb šîri, cf. ṭûbu); ištu Šamaš libbašu'issuxa *since Šamaš perverted his understanding* **6**, 8.—(2) *middle, midst,* and in this sense used with the prepositions ina, ana; ina libbi *in, among* **1**, 30; **2**, 2; **5**, 17; **18**, 7; ina libbi Upi'a *at Opis* **18**, 12; ina libbi *from, out of* **8**, 15; ina libbi balṭû *they live upon it* **2**, 45; ina libbi *in order that* **1**, 31; ina libbi ša *because* **6**, 23; ana libbi ša ana *until* **6**, 40.—(HW 367ᵃ)

libbû (=ina libbi); libbû (ša-bu-u) agâ *through, by means of, this* (measure) **4**, 24.—(HW 368ᵃ)

labâru, prt. ilbur, prs. ilábir *to be, to become, old:* infin. labâr (la-bar) pale *length of reign* **2**, 3; **3**, 3.—(HW 370ᵇ)

lakû *weak, miserable:* la-ku-u **14**, 9.—(HW 376ᵇ)

lalû *fulness, abundance:* lal-e balâṭi *fulness, enjoyment of life* **10**, 10.—(HW 377ᵃ)

lamû, prt. ilmî, *to surround, enclose, catch:* kî il-mu-u-ni *when they have caught* **2**, 51; ana muxxi dâkika il-mu-u *they have plotted* (tried to encompass) *thy destruction* **6**, 22.—(HW 379ᵃ)

lippu (لفّ *to wind, wrap up*) *bandage, dressing:* pl. lippe (li-ip-pi) **15**, r. 7.

lâšu (=lâ + išu, יֵשׁ) *there is not, there are not:* muššarâne la-aš-šu *there are no inscriptions* **16**, 20; çillâte la-aš-šu *there are no shelters* **17**, r. 1.—(HW 386ᵃ)

מ

ma, enclitic particle; draws the accent to the ultima of the word to which it is appended.—(1) Emphatic particle, minû iqabûní-ma *what, indeed, can they say* **6**, 30; šuxdû-ma ... lâ adûku *not willingly, indeed, could I have slain* **6**, 14; nindéma ilâni ... ippušû-ma *if only the gods will bestir themselves* **2**, 42; šûtú-ma *that* (*god*) *indeed* (here like ف in apodosis of conditional clause) **14**, 26; belijâ-ma *my lord* **5**, 6; ilâní-ma *the gods* **8**, r. 1; emurû-ma *they saw* **3**, 21.—(2) As conjunction, *and;* lilliká-ma *let him come and* **1**, 34; ša itûrá-ma *who returned and* **2**, 6; išemî-ma *he will hear and* **2**, 40, etc.—(HW 386ᵃ; 387ᵃ)

mâ *thus, as follows;* serves (like umma) to introduce direct discourse: ma-a 7, r. 6; 15, r. 4; 16, 19; 19, r. 5. 6.—(HW 387[b])

ma'adu *abundance, profusion:* dame ma-'a-du *much blood* (literally *blood a profusion*) 15, r. 6; zunnu ma'ada (ma-'a-da) *much rain* 16, r. 8.—(HW 389[b])

ma'âdu (מאד), prt. im'id, prs. imá'id, *to be much, numerous, abundant:* permans. ma'ada (ma-'a-da) *it is abundant* 17, r. 7.—(HW 388[a])

MU-GA, apparently an ideogram, 6, 39.

MU-GI, rab MU-GI *the chief m.*, an official title, 15, r. 3.

madâdu (מדד), prt. imdud, prs. imandad, *to measure.*—ℑ lumandid (lu-man-di-id) *let him measure out* (cf. bîrtu) 1, 35.—(HW 393[b])

mûdânûtu *science* (abstract of mûdânu, a formation in *-ân* (§ 65, No. 35) from mûdû *wise*, ידע): ina lâ mûdânûte (mu-da-nu-te) *unscientifically* (literally *without science*) 15, r. 8.

muxxu properly *top, summit* (Sumerian MUX), written muxxi, MUX. Usually combined with the prepositions ina, ana, ultu.—(1) ina muxxi; (a) *upon, over:* ina muxxi (MUX) naxnaxête ša appi *upon, over, the nostrils* 15, r. 9; ina muxxi (MUX) kâdu *over* (in command of) *the post* 3, r. 2. 12; ina muxxi (MUX) bît belika ul tašdud *thou hast not brought* (foe and famine) *upon thy lord's house* 6, 28.—(b) *against:* minû iqabûní-ma ina muxxi (MUX) ardu ša *what can they say against a servant who*, etc. 6, 30.—(c) *to:* ittalkûnu ina mux-xi-i̯a *they have come to me* 19, r. 4.—(d) *as to, in regard to:* 6, 4. 33; 12, 10; 15, r. 1.—(e) *for:* soldiers are sent ina muxxi (MUX) xalqûte *for, after, deserters* 7, 9; ina mux-xi napšâte ša belii̯a uçallâ *I pray for my lord's life* 13, r. 7.—(2) ana muxxi; (a) *towards, against:* ina libbi ana mux-xi-ni taráxuç *that you may feel confidence in* (towards) *us* 1, 32; emûqešu ana mux-xi-i-ni lâ išápar *that he may not send his troops against us* 2, 29; sîxa ana muxxi (MUX) U. *a rebellion against U.* 3, r. 17.—(b) *to, as far as:* ana muxxi (MUX) [al]Irgidû... kî itbû *when they reached Irgidu* 3, 11.—(c) *as to, in regard to:* 2, 33; 20, 11.—(d) *for:* ana muxxi (MUX) kurummâtini *for our provisions* (ye applied) 2, 53; ana muxxi (MUX) dâkika ilmû *they laid plans for thy destruction* 6, 21; ana muxxi (MUX) abii̯a *for,*

in behalf of, my father 20, 8.—(3) ultu muxxi *after, since:*
ultu muxxi (MUX) ša emurû-ma *after they saw* 3, 21; ultu
muxxi (MUX)... ikkiru *since, from the time that, he revolted*
4, 11.—(HW 398ª)

maxrû *former* (*Nisbeh* form): šarru maxrû (max-ru-u)
the former king 2, 5.—(HW 403ª)

maxâru, prt. imxur, prs. imáxar, properly *to be in front*
(cf. מָחָר *to-morrow*).—(1) *to receive, accept,* kî... maxru
(max-ru) *if it be acceptable, pleasing* 2, 32; 4, 27; šumma
maxir (ma-xi-ir) *same,* 15, r. 18.—(2) *to bring* (properly *to
place in front of*): tamáxarâní-ma (ta-max-xa-ra-nim-
ma) tanamdinânâšu *ye shall bring and give us* 2, 57.—(HW
400ᵇ)

maxîru (מָחִיר, properly *something received*) *price:* ana
maxîri (KI-LAM) *for sale* 1, 36.—(HW 404ᵇ)

mukîl, see kâlu.

mala (properly *fulness;* accus. of mâlu = mal'u, מְלָא,
written ma-la, never ma-la-a) *as much, many as:* ma-la
nišémû *all that we may hear* 1, 24; ma-la ibášû *all of them*
(literally *as many as exist*) 2, 12; 3, r. 5; ma-la dibbušu šulum *so far as* (as much as) *his words were propitious* 20, r. 4.—
(HW 410ᵇ)

malû (מְלָא) *full, complete:* zîmišu ma-la-a *his perfect
health* (literally *his full form*) 1, 14.—(HW 411ª)

mimma, minma (mîn + ma) *whatever, anything:* min-ma
anything 1, 36; ana mimma (NIN) kalâma *in regard to
everything whatever* 20, r. 3; mimma (NIN) ša... bîšu *whatever was bad* 5, 12.—(HW 418ᵇ.)   Cf. mî-nu, Eth. mî.

memeni (for man-man-ni) *any, any one:* ilânika šumma me-me-ni *if any of thy gods* 14, 24.   Cf. the following,
izirtû me-me-ni ina libbi šaṭrat *is any curse written
thereupon* H. 31, 10; dullu me-me-ni *any work* H. 109, r.
17; me-me-e-ni lû iš'alšu *nobody has asked him* II. 49, r.
23; ina muxxi me-me-ni lâ šalṭak *I have control over
nothing* (or *no one?*) H. 84, r. 6.—(HW 407ª)

mînu *how?* with ša, indefinite; mi-i-nu ša mâr šarri
beli išáparáni *as the prince may command* 8, r. 14.—(HW 406ᵇ)

mînû *what?* mi-nu-u 6, 29; mînâ-ma (mi-nam-ma) *why?*
2, 22; (me-nam-ma) *how?* 6, 5.—(HW 417ᵇ)

mindéma (cf. nindema) *when, if:* min (man)-di-e-ma
ana šarri beliia iqábî *if he says to the king* 5, r. 9.—Senn.

Bav. 40, arkiš min-di-ma Sin-axe-erba aggiš eziz-ma *afterwards when Sennacherib became violently enraged.*—(HW 416[a])

minma, cf. mimma.

maççartu (naçâru, נצר) *guard, watch* (both abstract and concrete): maççartâ'a (EN-NUN-a-a) ša taççurâ *the guard for me which ye have kept* 6, 37; ana ma-çar-ti lizzizû *let them stand guard* 7, r. 16; šulmu ana maççarâte (EN-NUN-MEŠ) gabbu *greeting to all the guards* 10, r. 5.—(HW 478[a])

maqâtu, prt. imqut, prs. imáqut *to fall.*—N[t] ittuqut (i-tu-qut, for intamqut, intauqut) *he fell* 11, r. 1.—(HW 424[a])

mâru *son:* written DU; mârušu ša *the son of* 1, 7; mâr axâti *nephew* (sister's son) 1, 8; 3, r. 1; mâre axi *nephews* (brother's sons) 3, 15; mâr mâre *grandchildren* 6, 40; mâre bânûti *free born citizens* (cf. banû) 3, 16; ilu mâr bîti *the god of* (son of) *the temple* 20, 10.—(HW 390[a])

marçu *sick, sick man, patient:* mar-çi 15, r. 1.—(HW 426[b])

marâçu (مرض) *to be sick, ill:* permans. maruç (ma-ru-uç) *he is ill* 1, 13.—(HW 426[a])

maruštu (fem. of maršu, properly *unclean*) *calamity, evil:* ma-ru-uš-ti 2, 18.—(HW 428[a])

mûšu (form like kûru, for muš'u), pl. mušâti (cf. مساء, مسى, Eth. *mĕsēt*), *night:* ûmi mu-šu *day and night* 13, r. 6. —(HW 429[b])

mašâ'u, prt. imšû', *to rob:* kurûmâtani ša mašâ' (ma-ša-') *our provisions which have been stolen* 2, 57.—(HW 428[a])

mašâru, I mušširu *to leave, abandon; to let go, set loose* (cf. Haupt in PAOS, March '94, cvi): mâtsunu ina kutallišunu muššurat (muš-šu-rat) *their country fell away* (was let loose) *from their side* 2, 20.—I[t] *to leave, abandon:* [âl]Madâkti undéšer (un-diš-šir) *he left* (abandoned) Madâktu 2, 7.—(HW 432[b])

muššarû, mušarû, musarû (from Sumerian MU *name* + SAR *to write*, Assyr. šiṭir šumi) *inscription:* muš-ša-ru-u 16, r. 3; pl. muššarâne (muš-ša-ra-ni-i) 16, 19.—(HW 421[a])

mâtu (Syr. ܡܬܐ) *land, country:* written KUR 1, 9; 2, 9; 7, 6, etc; ma-a-ti 4, 30; šar mâtâti (KUR-KUR) 3, 4; 4, 1. 4; 5, 1. 3, *king of the world* (literally *of the countries*).—(HW 434[b])

mâtu (מות), prt. imût, prs. imât, *to die:* permans. mîtu (mi-i-tu) *he died* 5, 16.—(HW 395[a])

mutîr-pûti (cf. pûtu, târu) *satellite:* [amel]GUR-RU-pu-tu 5, r. 25.—(HW 517[b])

נ

nîburu (עבר) *ferry:* ni-bu-ru 18, 13. r. 5. 13.—(HW 11[b], nîbiru.)

nâgiru, an official title, probably *overseer, superintendent:* [amel]LIGIR 2, 10.—(HW 447[b])

nadû, prt. iddî, prs. inádî, *to cast, cast down, lay:* ana tarçi axâmiš na-du-u *they are encamped* (lie) *opposite each other* 3, r. 23.—Ⓠ[t] qâtsunu ina libbi . . . it-ta-du-u *they put their hand upon* 3, r. 9.—(HW 448[b])

nadânu (נתן), prt. iddin, iddan; prs. inádin, inamdin, iddan, *to give, place.*—Prt. iddanakunušu (id-dan-nak-ku-nu-šu) *he used to give you* 2, 55; ana dâki iddinûka (id-din-u-ka) *they have given thee over to destruction* 6, 11; pîšunu iddanûnu (id-dan-nu-nu) *they sent a message* (literally *gave utterance*) 3, 25; niddinûni (ni-din-u-ni) *we gave* 15, 10.—Prs. addan (a-da-an) qâtâ'a *I will lay my hands* 7, r. 7; inamdinû (i-nam-di-nu) *they give* 2, 45; iddanû (id-dan-nu) *they will give* 13, r. 5; tanamdinânâšu (ta-nam-di-na-na-a-šu) *ye shall give us* 2, 58.—Prec. luddin (lu-ud-din) *I will give* 2, 28; liddinû (lid-di-nu) 14, 7; 15, 7; 17, 10; 19, 7; (lid-din-nu) 10, 12 *may they give;* niddin (ni-id-din) *we will give* (cohortative) 4, 32.—Ⓠ[t] ittedinšunu (it-ti-din-šu-nu) *he has given, sold, them* 19, r. 2; pîšu ittedin (it-ti-din) *he has given command* (properly *utterance*) 14, 27.—(HW 450[a])

nadâru, prt. iddur, *to lavish:* ana bel ṭâbâtešu id-dur *he used to lavish upon his partizans* 2, 47.—N and N[tn] *to be angry, rage.*—The stem may be compared to Syr. נְדַר *se profudit,* and so N and N[tn] would properly mean *to overflow;* cf. malî libbâti, libbâti imtalî, etc.—(HW 452[a])

nazâzu (Eth. nâzáza *to console,* properly *to support, to try to raise up, hold erect*), prt. izziz, prs. izzaz, *to stand:* elippu . . . ina Bâb-bitqi ta-za-az-za *the ship is* (stands) *at B-b.* 18, 10; ina pânia izzazû (i-za-zu) *they are* (stand) *with me* 7, r. 23; lizzizû (li-zi-zu) *let them stand* 7, r. 16.—Ⓠ[t] *to place one's self:* ittišu it-ta-ši-iz-zu (*i. e.* ittašizzû for ittazízû) *they have sided with him* 3, r. 20; ina muxxi amâtịa tattašizzâ (ta-at-ta-ši-iz-za-') *ye can bear witness to* (literally *take your stand upon*) *my words* 2, 31. In these forms the *š* for *z* is merely due to dissimilation.—(HW 455ᵃ)

naxnaxtu *ala of nostril* (cf. modern Arabic خنخ *to speak through the nose,*=خنخن, خنّ): pl. naxnaxête (na-ax-na-xi-e-te) ša appi 15, r. 10. Compare naxîru.

naxnaxûtu (na-ax-na-xu-tu) *breathing* 15, r. 11.

nixêsu, prt. ixxis, prs. ináxis, inamxis, *to retire, go back, go:* ana Elamti kî ix-xi-su *when they had gone to Elam* 5, 15; ana Elamti ul ix-xi-is *he has not gone to Elam* 5, r. 14.—(HW 458ᵃ)

naxîru (נְחִירָא) *nostril:* pî naxîre (na-xi-ri) *within the nostrils* 15, r. 14.—(HW 458ᵇ)

naxxartu (= namxartu, from maxâru *to receive*) *receipt, income:* na-xar-tu 17, 13.—(HW 405ᵇ, namxurtu)

nakru *foe, enemy:* nakru (ᵃᵐᵉˡ KUR) u bûbûtu *foe and famine* 6, 27.—(HW 465ᵃ)

nakâru (נכר), prt. ikkir, *to be strange, hostile; to revolt:* ina qât šarri ik-ki-ru (mod. rel.) *he revolted from the king* 4, 13.—(HW 464ᵇ)

nîmélu (properly *result of labor,* עמל, عمل) *produce, gain; welfare:* ni-me-il-šu *his welfare* 12, r. 1.—(HW 83ᵇ)

nîni (نحن) *we:* ni-i-[ni]? 18, 15; cf. anîni.

nindéma (= mindéma, with assimilation of *m* to *n*) *if:* nin-di-e-ma . . . iqábî *if the king thinks* 2, 36; nin-di-e-ma . . . ippušû-ma *if they will bestir themselves* 2, 41.

nasâxu, prt. issux, prs. inásax, *to pluck, tear out, remove with violence:* libbašu issuxa (ZI-xa) *took away his understanding* 6, 8.—(HW 471ᵃ)

nasîku (נסיך) *prince:* ᵃᵐᵉˡna-si-ku 3, 14; pl. nasîkâti (ᵃᵐᵉˡna-si-ka-a-ti) *authorities, rulers* 3, 19.—(HW 472ᵇ)

napištu (נפש, نفس) *soul, life,* properly *breath:* pl. napša-a-te 8, r. 11. 18; ZI-MEŠ 13, r. 7 *life;* [balâṭ] na-piš-ti 13, r. 1–2; balâṭ napšâte (TIN ZI-MEŠ) 4, 6; 5, 6; 20, 5 *life;* VII napšâte (ZI-MEŠ) šunu *they are seven in number* (literally *seven souls*) 19, r. 1.—(HW 476ᵃ)

naçâru (נצר, نظر), prt. iççur, prs. ináçar, *watch, keep, protect:* 2 pl. taççurâ (taç-çu[r-ra]) 6, 37.—Prec. 3 pl. liççurû (li-iç-çu-ru) 8, r. 19.—Impv. sg. uçrî (uç-ri) 4, 37; pl. uçrâ (uç-ra) 3, 8.—(HW 477ᵃ)

niqû (properly *libation*, naqû *to pour out;* cf. מִנְקִיּוֹת) *offering, sacrifice:* written LU-SIGISSE 8, 18. r. 6.—(HW 479[b])

nâru (נהר, نَهْر) *river:* written ID 2, 9; 3, r. 22.—(HW 440[a])

nišu, pl. niše (אנוש, ناس), *people:* written UN, UN-MEŠ; niše (UN-MEŠ) bîtini the people of our house 2, 55; niše (UN-MEŠ) ša ina Ninua the people of Nineveh 9, r. 5. As determinative before gentilic names, *passim*.—(HW 483[a])

našû (נשא), prt. iššî, prs. inášî, *to lift, carry, bring, take:* iššâ (iš-ša-') 5, 19. 20; iššâ-ma (iš-šam-ma) 5, r. 12 *he brought;* ša . . . iš-šu-u *whom he got* 19, r. 1; rešni ni-iš-ši (cohortative) *we will hold up our heads* 17, r. 5.—Part. nâši, cstr. nâš; nâš šappâte (ŠAMAN-LAL-MEŠ) *jar bearers* 8, r. 6.—𝔑[t] ittanášû (it-tan-na-aš-šu) *they levy, collect* 2, 50.—(HW 484[a])

našpartu (šapâru) *command, behest:* na-aš-par-tu ša šarri *the king's behest* 4, 22.—(HW 683[b])

ס

sebû (سابِع) *seventh:* ûmu sebû (VII KAM) *the seventh day* 11, 6.—(HW 489[b])

sâdu *pasture*(?): sa-a-du 1, 31, 39; see parâku, p. 76.

sîxu (for six'u) *revolt:* si-xu ana muxxi U. *a revolt against U.* 3, r. 17.—(HW 492[b])

saxû *to revolt:* sîxû (si-xu) šunûti *they are in a state of revolt* 2, 22.—(HW 492[b]). The *i* intrans. as in çibû.

saxâru (סחר), prt. isxur, *to turn* (intransitive).—𝔍[t] *to return, bring back:* ilu . . . ussaxxar (u-sa-ax-xar, cf. § 51, 2) *he will bring the god back* 8, r. 3.—(HW 494[a])

sikiptu (sakâpu) *overthrow, defeat;* as a term of reproach, *smitten, accursed* (cf. kibistu): si-kip-ti Bel *accursed of Bel* 2, 39; si-kip-ti Marduk agâ K 84 (II 301), r. 17; si-kip-ti Bel arrat ilâni *smitten of Bel accursed of the gods* K. 1250 (SK., ii. 59), 14.—(HW 499[a])

sikru (= zikru, cf. sikru = zikru *name, command*, etc., partial assimilation of initial *z* to following *k;* placed in HW sub סכר and זכר respectively) *man:* lakû si-ik-ru xanni'u *that poor fellow* 14, 10.

sunqu (sanâqu *to squeeze, press;* Syr. סנק *to need*) *need, famine:* su-un-qu 2, 19.—(HW 505[b])

פ

pû (פה, فو), genitive pî, *mouth*, then *utterance*, *word:* pi-i naxîre *within* (properly *in the mouth of*, فى) *the nostrils* 15, r. 14; pi-i-šu-nu iddanûnu *they sent a message* (literally *gave their utterance*) 3, 24; pi-i-šu ittedin *he has given his command* 14, 27.—(HW 523ª.) Cf. pânu, pânâtu, pûtu.

paxâru, prt. ipxur, *to gather, assemble* (intransitive): mât Akkadî ni-ip-xur-ma *we, all Babylonia, will assemble* 4, 29.—𝕴 transitive: bel ṭâbâtešu gabbi kî u-pax-xir *having assembled all his adherents* 2, 24; emûqešu kî u-pax-xir *having assembled his forces* 3, r. 21; u-pax-xa-ru-ma *they collect* 2, 44.—(HW 520ª)

paxâtu (pexû *to close, shut in*) *district*, then for bel paxâti *governor* (פחה): amel EN-NAM, bel paxâti or simply paxâtu 5, 19; 18, 11. r. 2; 19, 9.—(HW 519ᵇ)

paṭâru (פטר), prt. ipṭur, prs. ipâṭar, *to break, cleave, loose.* —𝕼ᵗ širṭu ap-ta-ṭar *I undid the bandage* 14, 18.—(HW 522ª)

palû *regnal year, reign:* labâr pale (BAL-e) *length of reign* 2, 3; 3, 4.—(HW 525ª)

palâxu (Syr. פלח *to reverence, serve*), prt. iplax, prs. ipálax, *to fear, be afraid:* k[î ip]-la-xu (sg.) 2, 7; kî ip-la-xu (pl.) 3, 24 *having become alarmed.*—(HW 525ᵇ)

puluxtu *fear, terror, panic:* ina pu-lux-ti *in a state of panic* 2, 16; pu-lux-ti ulteribû *they are invaded by panic* 2, 18.—(HW 526ᵇ)

pânu (פנים, properly old plural of pû).—(1) *face:* pa-ni-šu-nu ana âl Š. šaknû *their faces turned towards* (i. e., going in the direction of) *Š.* 2, 13.—(2) *front, presence:* ina pânija (ŠI-ja) izzazû *they are with me* (stand in my presence) 7, r. 22; ina pa-ni . . . qibî *tell* (say in the presence of) 19, r. 5; ina pa-an šarri lîrubû *let them come into the king's presence* 16, 10; qaqqar ina pa-ni-šu-nu rûqu *a long stretch of ground lay in front of them* 3, 17; ina pa-ni dâku *for the purpose of killing* 4, 14; kî ina pa-ni šarri maxru 4, 26; šumma pa-an šarri maxir 15, r. 18 *if it be acceptable to* (before) *the king* (cf. 2, 32); ana pa-ni-šu-nu ašápar *I will send to them* 2, 38; kî . . . ana pa-ni-šu-nu ittalka *when he reaches them* (comes into their presence) 2, 39.—(HW 530ª)

pânâtu (fem. pl. of pânu) *front* (of space and time): ina pa-na-tu *beforehand* 7, 20.—(HW 531ᵇ)

paqâdu (פקד), prt. ipqid, prs. ipáqid, *to command, appoint:* ša . . . ap-ki-du *whom I had appointed* 3, r. 3; šulmu issika . . . lipqidû (lip-qi-du) *may they ordain prosperity with thee* 9, r. 10.—(HW 534b)

parâku, prt. iprik, prs. ipárik, *to separate, shut off, lock.*—Qt kî . . . išten immeru ana sâdu ša Elamti ip-te-ir-ku (*constructio praegnans*) *if a single sheep* (is separated from your flocks and) *gets over to the Elamite pasture*(?) 1, 40.—(HW 539b)

parâsu, prt. iprus, prs. ipáras, *to decide* (properly *to cut*): ana pa-ra-su ša šarnuppi inamdinû *they place* (the grain) *under the charge* (subject to the decision) *of the šarnuppu* 2, 44; similarly pa-ra-su ša šarnuppi 2, 48.—(HW 542b)

parap *five-sixths:* parap (KINGUSILI) kaspu *five-sixths of a shekel* 15, 10.—(HW 538a, parab)

parçu (فَرْض) *command, ordinance:* pl. parçe (pa-ar-çi) ša ilâni *the commands of the gods* 8, r. 10.—(ḤW 544b)

paširâti (properly *explanation;* pašâru *to loose, solve;* פשרא) *guarantee, credentials:* pa-ši-rat-ti . . . lušebilšu *I will send it* (the royal signet) *as a guarantee* (i. e., to give force to my request) 2, 35; šipirtâ pa-ši-rat-ti . . . ašápar *I will send my* (simple) *message as a guarantee* (i. e., my message will be guarantee enough for them) 2, 37.

pûtu (fem. of pû), *front, entrance, border:* mutîr-pûtu (amel GUR-RU pu-tu) *satellite, body-guard* (properly he who stood at the entrance and turned back those approaching) 5, r. 25.—(HW 517ab)

pittu (for pit'u, פתע) *moment, twinkling;* only in adverbial expressions ina pitti, appittma (=ana pitti-ma), etc.: ina pi-it-ti *immediately* 16, r. 5.—(HW 553a)

צ

çâbu (for çabbu, çab'u; ضَبأ) *man, soldier:* pl. çâbe, written ERIM-MEŠ 3, 6; amel ERIM-MEŠ 7, 7. 12. r. 2. 5. 9; çâbêja (amel ERIM-MEŠ-ja) *my men* 7, r. 19.—(HW 557b)

çibû (Aram. צְבָא) *to wish, desire:* kî . . . çi-bu-u *if he wishes* 5, r. 15. The *i* in çibû is the intransitive *i* as in çixru *small* = çaxir, Arabic نِجْس nijs *unclean* = najis, etc. (Barth, § 21).—(HW 558b)

çabâtu (צבט, where ט is due to influence of צ) *to grasp, seize, take:* kî iç-ba-tu *when he received* 2, 47; qâtsu kî aç-ba-tu *when I had taken his hand* (i. e., taken him under my protection) 1, 12; adî zîmišu malâ içábatu (i-çab-ba-tu) *as soon as he regains complete health* 1, 15; içábatû-ma (i-çab-ba-tu-ma), *they will seize him and* 2, 42; ana muxxi ça-ba-ta (infin.) *with reference to the capture* 2, 33; širṭu ša ina libbi ça-bit-u-ni (permans.) *the bandage which held it on* 14, 18.—Q¹ *to seize, take:* iç-çab-tu *they seize* 2, 53; ade . . . iç-çab-tu *they made terms* (undertook agreements) 3, r. 3; adannu ša šulum adî ûmi rebî iç-çab-ta *he fixed on* (took) *the* (literally *up to the*) *fourth day as the propitious occasion* 20, r. 2. —S xi'lânu tu-ša-aç-bat-ma (ellipsis of xarrânu) *put troops upon the march* 4, 9.—(HW 560ᵃ)

çibûtu *wish, desire:* ana çi-bu-tu bel šarrâni *in accordance with the wish of the lord of kings* 2, 60.—(HW 559ᵃ)

çixru (for çaxiru, çaxru, صغر = صغر, fem. çaxirtu and çixirtu) *little, small:* ubâni çi-xi-ir-te *the little finger* 14, 23.—(HW 565ᵃ)

çullû (صلّى) *to pray:* 1 sg. u-çal-lu 4, 7; u-çal-li 5, 7; 20, 6; u-çal-la 13, r. 9 *I pray.*—(HW 567ᵃ)

çillatu (צל, ظلّ) *shelter, cover:* pl. çi-il-la-a-te *shelters* (for storage of wine) 17, 15.

çâtu (properly pl. of çîtu, צאת; açû *to go out*) *exit, end:* ana ça-at ûme *to the end of time* 8, r. 21.—(HW 239ᵇ)

ק

QA, a measure: ana I QA A-AN X BAR A-AN *ten* BAR *for one* QA 2, 56; I QA aklišu *one* QA *of his food* 8, r. 8.

qebû (Aram. קבע *to fix*[?]), prt. iqbî, prs. iqábî *to say, speak, command.*—Prt. ša . . . aq-bu-u-nu, *whom I mentioned* 16, 7; amât ša . . . aqbâkunušu (aq-bak-ku-nu-šu) *the word which I spoke to you* 2, 27.—Prs. lâ aqábûšunu (a-qa-ba-aš-šu-nu) *I do not tell them* 16, 15; mindéma iqábî (i-qa-bi) *if he says* 5, r. 9; nindéma šarru i-qab-bi *if the king thinks* (says to himself) 2, 36; minâ-ma . . . iqábâ-ma (i-qab-ba-am-ma) *how can he speak* 6, 6; i-qab-bu-u *they say* 2, 14; minû iqábûní-ma (i-qab-bu-nim-ma) *what can they say?* 6, 30.—Prec. šarru li-qab-bi (prs. Qal, or Piel?) *let the king give orders* 17, r. 3; liq-bu-u *may they com-*

mand 1, 6; 5, r. 21.—Imv. fem. qi-bi-' *say!* 19, r. 5.—𝔔t iq-ṭe-bi-a *he says* 15, r. 4; iqtabûnîšu (iq-ta-bu-niš-šu) *they said to him* 1, 28.—(HW 577a)

qallu *servant, slave:* written ^{amel}GAL-LA 5, r. 7. 16.—(HW 585b)

qinnu (קן) *nest, family:* ^{amel}qin-na-aš-šu gabbi *all his family* 2, 8.—(HW 588b)

qâpu, prt. iqîp, prs. iqâp *to believe, trust, entrust.*—Prs. šarru lâ i-qâp-šu *let not the king believe him* 5, r. 11; 1. a-qip-pu-' (§ 115) *I believe* 6, 32.—𝔍 ša u-ka-ip-[u]-ni *who have appointed, put in charge* 7, r. 13.—(HW 583b)

qiçru (qaçâru *to bind*) *band, battalion:* rabe-qiçir (^{amel}GAL-ki-çir-MEŠ) *chiefs of battalion, majors* 7, 10. r. 3.—(HW 591b)

qaqqadu (קדקד) *head, top, tip:* qaqqad (SAG-DU) ubâni çixirti *the tip of the little finger* 14, 22.—(HW 592b)

qarâdu, prt. iq-ri-dan-nu 3, r. 13.

qarçu *piece:* qarçu akâlu (Syr. אכל קרצא) *to slander, calumniate* (properly *to eat the pieces*)*:* qar-çi-ka ina pânîja ekulu *he slandered thee before me* 6, 9.—(HW 597b)

qâšu, prt. iqîš *to grant, bestow:* liqîšû (li-ki-šu) *may they grant* 2, 4; 3, 5.—(HW 584b)

qaštu (קשת), pl. qašâti.—(1) *bow:* ina qašti (GIŠ-PAN) ramîti *with bow relaxed, unstrung* 2, 42 (cf. קשת רמיה, Ps. lxxviii. 57; Hos. vii. 16).—(2) *force, troops:* qašta (GIŠ-PAN) šunu mâla ibášû kî idqû *having mustered their entire force* 3, r. 4.—(HW 598a)

qâtu, dual. qâtâ, *hand:* qa-ta-a-a (i. e. qâtâ'a) *my hands* 7, r. 8; elsewhere written ŠU; ša ina qât D. . . . nušebila *which* (i. e. the letters) *we sent by* (ביד) *D.* 5, r. 23; ina qât dîkîtu *accompanied by a troop* 2, 38; kunukku ina qâtišunu *provided with a warrant* 7, 8; qâtsu kî açbata *having taken his hand* (i. e. given him my protection) 1, 12; ina qât *from* 1, 27; 2, 60.—(HW 598b)

qatû *to come to an end, perish:* 2 sg. permans. qatâta, ina libbi ša itti bît belika qa-ta-a-ta *because thou wouldst have perished with thy lord's house* 6, 19.—(HW 599b)

ר

rabû (רב), cstr. rab, *great:* rab bîti (^{amel}GAL E) *majordomo* 2, 52; rab qiçir (cf. qiçru) *chief of battalion, major* 7, 10. r. 3; rab MU-GI 15, r. 3.—(HW 609a)

rubû (cf. rabû) *magnate, noble:* rubešu (amel GAL-MEŠ-šu) *his nobles* **2**, 40.—(HW 610ª)

rebû (ربع) *fourth:* ûmu rebû (IV-KAM) *the fourth day* (of the month) **8**, 10; **12**, r. 6; **20**, r. 2.—(HW 608ª)

rîxu *remaining, the rest of:* pl. rîxûte (ri-xu-te) *the rest* (of the inscriptions, muššarâni) **16**, r. 5.—(HW 618ᵇ)

raxâçu (התרחצו, Dan. iii. 28), prt. irxuç, prs. iráxuç, *to trust, to have confidence in:* ina libbi ana muxxini tara-ax-xu-uç *in order that you may have confidence in us* **1**, 32.—(HW 617ª)

rixtu (stem رخ ?) pl. rixâti and rixêti, *salutation, greeting:* ri-xa-a-te ša Nabû *greetings from Nabû* **10**, r. 1.—(HW 616ª)

rakâsu (רכס, ركس), prt. irkus, *to bind.*—**Ɪ**ᵗ tal'îtu ina muxxi urtakkis (ur-ta-ki-is) *I had applied* (bound on) *a dressing* **14**, 13.—(HW 620ᵇ)

râmu (רחם, رحم), prt. irâm, irem, prs. irâm *to love:* ardu ša bît belišu i-ram-mu *a servant who loves his lord's house* **6**, 31;—prt. râ'imu (ra-'-i-mu) *loving* **2**, 62.—(HW 603ᵇ)

remu (for raḥmu) *grace, favor, mercy:* remu (ri-mu) aškunáka *I have shown thee favor* **6**, 24.—(HW 604ª)

ramû (רמה, رمى), prt. irmî, *to throw, throw down, lay;* intrans. *to be slack, relaxed.*—**Ɪ** šubat çabe rammî (ra-amme, impv.) *establish a military post* **1**, r. 6.—(HW 622ª)

ramû *relaxed:* ina qašti ramîti (ra-mi-ti) *with bow relaxed, unstrung* (cf. qaštu) **2**, 42.—(HW 623ª)

râmânu (properly *highness*, רום) *self:* ra-man-šu *himself* **2**, 41.—(HW 624ª)

râqu (רחק), prt. irîq, *to be, or become, distant; to depart:* lillikû dullašunu lîpušû li-ri-qu-u-ni *let them come, perform their duty, and depart* H. **386**, r. 3–5.—**Ɪ** Ašur urâqannî-ma (u-raq-an-ni-i-ma) *Ašur withholds me, keeps me far from* **6**, 13.—(HW 605ᵇ)

rûqu (רחוק) *distant, remote:* qaqqar ina pânišunu ru-u-qu *they had a long stretch of ground before them* **3**, 18; [ûme] ru-qu-u-te *distant days* **13**, r. 3.—(HW 605ᵇ)

rešu (ראש, رأس).—(1) *head:* rešni (ri-[iš]-ni) niššî *we will lift up our heads* (be all right) **17**, r. 5.—(2) *officer:* written amel SAG, **19**, r. 8; pl. amel SAG-MEŠ **7**, 7. r. 1.—(HW 606ª)

ratâmu (רתם), prt. irtum, *to bind, wrap:* ina appišu ir-tu-mu (which) *covered* (enveloped) *his face* (nose) **14**, 14.

ש

ša (originally šâ, and properly "accusative" of šû *he*).—(1) Demonstrative pronoun, *that one, those:* [amel]Puqûdu ša ina [al]T. *the Pukudeans* (*viz.*) *those in T.* **1**, 19; înâšu ša kûri *his eyes are diseased* (those of disease, like ذو with genit.) **14**, 11; ša bitxallâti *the cavalry* (they of riding horses) **7**, r. 22.—(2) Relative pronoun, *who, which*, for all genders, numbers and cases: **2**, 5. 23. 57. 60; **3**, 15; **5**, 12; **16**, 6, etc.—(3) Preposition, sign of the genitive, *of*, **1**, 5. 7. 8; **2**, 4. 16. 38. 45; **3**, 6. 13. 14; **10**, r. 7; **11**, 9. etc.; (as further development of this usage) *from*, ša libbi adri ekalli *from the palace enclosure* (he will go, etc. **8**, 16; dâme ša appišu illakûni *blood comes from his nose* **15**, r. 2.—(4) Conjunction, *that:* apil šipri ibâšu ša *a messenger has come to him* (with the news) *that* **1**, 17.—(5) Used in a variety of compound expressions; ina libbi ša *because* **6**, 17. 23; adî ša *until* **5**, r. 13; ultu muxxi ša *since, after* **3**, 21; **4**, 11–12; kî ša *as* **4**, 34; *how* **5**, r. 20; *if* **5**, r. 21–22.—(HW 630[a])

šû.—(1) Pers. pronoun, *he*, fem. šî *she*, pl. masc. šunu, šun, fem. šina, *they;* šu-u *he* **5**, 9. 11. 17; **6**, 20; šu-nu *they* **2**, 37; **7**, r. 7. 22; **8**, r. 10; **19**, r. 1.—(2) Demons. pronoun, *this, that*, pl. šunûti(u), fem. šinâti, šinâtina: elippu ši-i *that ship* **18**, 6; šu-u eteqa illaka *this is the route he will follow* **8**, r. 4; sîxû šu-nu-tu *these* (people) *are in revolt* **2**, 22; šu-nu-ti-ma . . . liqbû *let these* (men) *tell* **5**, r. 19.—(HW 645[a])

še'u *grain, corn:* še' (ŠE-BAR) šibši (cf. šibšu) **2**, 43. 48.—(HW 631[a])

ša'âlu (שׁאל, سأل), prt. iš'al, prs. išâ'al, *to ask, inquire:* a-ša-'al *I will make inquiries* **7**, r. 6; kî aš-'-a-lu *when I asked* **20**, 13; liš-'-al *let him question* **5**, r. 26; liš-'-al-šu *let some one* (subject indefinite) *question him* **3**, r. 25.—(HW 633[a])

ši'âru, šeru (שַׁחַר) *morning, morrow:* ina ši-a-ri *tomorrow* **15**, r. 18.—(HW 635[a])

šabâṭu *Shebat*, the eleventh month of the Babylonian calendar: written ITI-AŠ, **8**, r. 16.—(HW 638[a])

šibsu *tax, impost, rent,* apparently paid in kind: še šib-ši *tax-corn, grain levied as an impost* 2, 43; še' agâ ša šib-ši *this tax-corn* 2, 48; si-ib-šu eqli *the rent of a field* Str. Nbn. 167, 2; 753, 9.—Cf. KB. iv. 53 n.

šubtu (ašâbu, ישב), cstr. šubat.—(1) *dwelling, settlement:* šubat (KU) çâbe *a military post* 7, r. 5.—(2) *ambush:* šu-ub-tu ina pânâtu ussešibu *he had laid an ambush beforehand* 7, 20.—(HW 246ª; AJSL. xiv. 3)

šadâdu, prt. išdud, ildud, *to draw, bring:* mât Elamti ildudá-ma (il-du-da-am-ma) *brought on Elam* (against us) 4, 13; nakru u bûbûti.... ul taš-du-ud *foe and famine thou hast not brought on* 6, 29.—(HW 64ª)

šuxdû (from xadû; form like šurbû, šušqû, §65, No. 33b) *glad, willing:* šu-ux-du-u-ma.... lâ *not willingly* 16, 14.

šaṭâru (שטר, سطر), prt. išṭur, prs. išâṭar, *to write:* kî ša šaṭrâ (šaṭ-ra) *how they* (the letters) *were written* 5, r. 20; lišṭurû (liš-ṭu-ru) *let them write* 16, r. 4. 6.—(HW 651ᵇ)

šaknu (šakânu).—(1) *deputy, lieutenant:* šaknûtišunu (amel ŠA-nu-MEŠ-šu-nu) *their deputies* 7, r. 13; ša-ak-nu Bel *the deputy, representative, of Bel,* Sarg. Cyl. 1.—(2) *governor,* i. e. the deputy of the king.—(HW 659ᵇ)

šakânu (שכן, سكن), prt. iškun, prs. išákan, *to place, make, do.*—Prt. remu aškunáka (aš-kun-ak-ka) *I have shown thee favor* 6, 25; xamaṭṭa iškununi (ŠA-nu-u-ni) *they rendered aid* 8, r. 17; lâ niš-kun *we could not place* 16, r. 1.—Prs. i-šak-kan 2, 65; nišákanúni *we would (like to) place* 17, r. 2.—Prec. liškunû (liš-ku-nu) *let them place* 15, r. 15; 16, r. 7; âka ni-iš-kun *where shall we place?* 17, r. 8.—Permans., pânišunu ana alŠ. šaknû (šak-nu) *with their faces turned towards Š.* (circumstantial clause) 2, 13–14.—Nᵗ itti sunqu ina mâtišunu it-taš-kin *when need came (was laid) upon their land* 2, 19.—(HW 657ª)

šelibu (ثعلب, ثعال, שועל), *fox:* written LUB-A 11, 7.—(HW 634ᵇ)

šulmu (šalâmu), cstr. šulum, *welfare, prosperity:* usually written DI-mu; sulmu.... lipqidû *may they ordain prosperity* 9, r. 4. 7; adannu ša šu-lum *the propitious occasion* 20, r. 1; mâla dibbušu šu-lum *so far as his words were favorable* 20, r. 5; šulmu iâši *it is well with me* 6, 2; šulmu adanniš *all goes well* 14, 8. 28.—Especially frequent in formulas of greeting, šulmu, šulmu adanniš, ana šarri, etc., *greeting* (welfare), *a hearty greeting* (welfare exceedingly) *to the king*, etc., **7**, 3. 5; **8**, 3; **9**, 4; **12**, 5; **13**, 3; **14**, 3, etc.—(HW 664b)

šalâmu (שלם, سلم), prt. išlim, prs. išâlim, *to be whole, complete, perfect.*—𝔓 našparta ša šarri u-šal-lam *I will fulfill the king's command* **4**, 23; lu-šal-li-mu-ka *may they keep thee whole* **9**, 10; lu-šal-li-mu lîpušû *may they perfectly perform* **8**, r. 13.—(HW 663b)

šâlšu (ثالث), ordinal number, *third:* ûmu šâlšu (III KAM) *the third day* **8**, 7.—(HW 666b)

šumu (שם, اسم, stem ושם), pl. šumâte (שמות), *name:* šu-mu ili *the name of the god* **1**, 22.—(HW 666b)

šemû (שמע, سمع), prt. išmî, prs. išémî, *to hear:* išémîma (i-šim-mi-e-ma) *he will hear and* **2**, 40; ašémîš (a-šim-meš) *I will hear it* **6**, 7; mâla nišémû (ni-šim-mu-u) *as much as we may hear* **1**, 24; šulmû lašmî (la-aš-me) *let me he hear* (*his*) *welfare* (i. e. how he does) **15**, r. 19.—𝔑^{t} tattašmâ'innî (ta(?)-taš-ma-in-ni) *ye heard me* **2**, 30. Harper, following Pinches (IV^{2}, **52**, No. 2), reads the first character, conjecturally, ri, tal, but some form of šemû is clearly required here.—𝔖 ul ušašmû (u-ša-aš-mu) *I have not informed* (or prs.?) **2**, 62.—(HW 667a)

šummu *if:* šum-mu **7**, r. 7; šum-ma **14**, 24; **15**, r. 18.—(HW 670b)

šunu *they*, cf. šû.

šânû (for šâni'u, šâniịu), ordinal number, *second:* **ûmu šânû** (II KAM) *the second day* **12**, r. 5.—(HW 674b)

šinâ (שנים) *two:* šinâ (II-TA) agâ šanâte *these two years* **6**, 26.—(HW 674b)

šunûti *they, those*, cf. šû.

šupâlu (שפל, سفل) *lower part:* for ana šu-pal šâru **2**, 9, rendered *southward*, cf. tâmtim šaplîtu as applied to the Persian Gulf, Zâba šaplîtu the Lower Zab, etc.; šupâl šâri would be a construct relation (like أَوَّلُ بَيْتٍ), meaning literally *the lower* (i. e. the southern) *wind.*—(HW 681b)

šipru (cf. Heb. ספר *message, letter, writing, book;* ספר is an Assyrian loanword, therefore ס for *š*) *message:* apil šipri (amel A-KIN) *messenger* **1**, 17. 33; **2**, 38; **4**, 27; **16**, 8.—(HW 683a)

šapâru (سفر, سافر, *to set out, journey*), prt. išpur, prs. išâpar, *to send, send word*, often with idea of command implied.—Prt. iš-pu-ra 4, 8; iš-[pu-ra-ni] 4, 21; 2. taš-pur 6, 5. 35; 1. aš-pu-ra 3, r. 24.—Prs. sg. i-šap-par 2, 29; 16, 16; i-šap-par-an-ni *sends to command me* 8, r. 15; 2. ta-šap-par 4, 10; 1. a-šap-par 2, 38; ašáparášu (a-šap-pa-raš-šu) *I will send him* 1, 16; pl. išáparûníšu (i-šap-pa-ru-niš-šu) *they will send him* 2, 43; 1. nišáparáka (ni-šap-pa-rak-ka) *we will send to thee* 1, 25.—Prec. liš-pu-ra *let him send orders* 7, r. 14.—Ⅎt *same:* issapra (i-sap-ra) 16, 18; 2. tal-tap-ra 1, 37; 1. assapra (a-sap-ra) 16, r. 3; al-tap-ra 1, 42; 3, 7. r. 14; 4, 33; 5, r. 27; assaparšunu (a-sa-par-šu-nu) *I sent them* 7, 10; assaprašunu (a-sap-ra-šu-nu) *I send, have sent, them* 16, 9; assaparášunu (a-sa-par-aš-šu-nu) *I sent word to them* 7, r. 5.—(HW 682a)

The primitive meaning of the stem šapâru may be *to be swift*, transit. *to dispatch;* šapparu *wild goat* (whence שׁוֹפָר) may be *the swift one;* see Proc. Am. Or. Soc., Oct. '98, p. clxxv, n. 4; Report of the U. S. National Museum for 1892, pp. 437–450.

šipirtu (fem. of šipru) *message, letter:* šipirtâ (ši-pir-ta-a) *my message* 2, 37; pl. šipirêti (ši-pir-e-ti) *letters* 5, 17. 19. r. 12. 19. 22.—(HW 683b)

šappatu, pl. šappâte (better, perhaps, sappatu; cf. Heb. סַפּוֹת *basins, dishes*), *jar:* nâš-šappâte (amel ŠAMAN-LAL-MEŠ) *jar-bearers* 8, r. 6; for the ideogram ŠAMAN cf. Be. 1, (PSBA. Dec. '88) Col. I., 6.—(HW 681b)

šâru (שַׂעַר, שְׂעָרָה) *wind.*—(1) *point of the compass:* ana šupâl ša-a-ru *southward* (cf. šupâlu) 2, 19.—(2) *air:* ša-a-ru ikkasir *the air will be kept away* 15, r. 15.—(HW 635b)

šîru (שְׁאֵר) pl. šîrê *flesh, body:* ṭûb šîri (UZU) *welfare, health of body* 1, 5; 2, 2; ṭûb šîre (UZU-MEŠ) 3, 3; 10, 9; 14, 6; 15, 6; 19, 7.—(HW 634b)

šarru (שַׂר), cstr. šar, pl. šarrâni, *king:* written LUGAL 1, 15; 2, 5. 28, etc.;—pl. LUGAL-MEŠ 1, 1. 5; 2, 1. 3. etc.;—mâr šarri (DU LUGAL) *prince* 8, 1. 3. 5. 11. r. 12. 14. 18; 10, 1. 3. 11. r. 3. 7; 15, 8.—(HW 692b)

širṭu (properly *strip;* šarâṭu *to tear, cut,* שׂרט, شرط) *bandage:* ši-ir-ṭu 14, 17.—(HW 690b)

šarku *pus:* šar-ku 14, 20.—(HW 692a, sub שׁרק)

šarnuppu, Elamite official title: amel ša-ar-nu-up-pu 2, 45; amel ša-ar-nu-up-pi 2, 48, 51.

šârâte (fem. plural of šâru *wind,* = *Windbeuteleien?*) *lies, treason:* šipirêti agâ ša ša-ra-a-ti *these treasonable letters* 5, r. 20; ša-ra-te-e-šu (i. e. šârâtéšu) lâ tašémâ *do not listen to his lies* H. 301, 19.—(HW 648a)

šarrûtu (abstract from šarru) *royalty, sovereignty:* šar-ru-ut-ka *thy sovereignty* 8, r. 20.—(HW 693a)

šûtu *he, that one:* šu-tu-ma *that* (god) *indeed* 14, 26.—(HW 648b)

šattu (for šantu, שָׁנָה, سنة) *year:* pl. šanâte (MU-AN-NA-MEŠ) 5, 8; 6, 26; 17, 8.—(HW 673a)

ת

tebû (تبع *to follow*), prt. itbî, prs. itábî, itébî, *to march, go* (especially with hostile intent): kî it-bû-u *when they came* (had marched) 3, 13; it-[bu-u-ni] *they marched* 3, r. 7; tibânu tebâ (ti-ba-') *make ye a raid!* 3, 9.—Qtn it-te-ni-ib-bu-u *they had come* (marched) 3, 23.—(HW 698b)

tibnu (תֶּבֶן, تبن) *straw:* written ŠE-IN-NU 18, 15. r. 8.—(HW 700b)

tîbânu (tebânu) *raid, incursion* (tebû): ti-ba-a-nu tebâ *made ye a raid* 3, 9.

taziru, an official title: amel ta-zi-ru 7, r. 11.

tal'îtu (stem לאי?) *(surgical) dressing*: ta-al-i-tu 14, 12. 19; ta-al-i-te 14, 21.—(HW 366a)

tullummâ'u, apparently a term of reproach; šunu tul-lu-um-ma-'-u *they are . . .*, 2, 37.

timâli, itimâli (אתמול) *yesterday:* ina ti-ma-li 14, 15; 15, r. 5.—(HW 158a)

tapšuru (pašâru) *ransom:* tap-šu-ru igámar-ma *he will pay a ransom* 2, 40.

târu (תור *to spy out*, properly *to go about*, like سار), prt. itûr, prs. itâru, *to turn, return:* ša . . . . [i-tu-ra]-am-ma (i. e. itûrá-ma) *who returned* 2, 6; ûmu rebû târšu (GUR-šu) ša Nabû *on the fourth day* (*will take place*) *the return of Nabû* 8, 10.—J Transitive, utâráka (u-tar-rak-ka *I will return to thee, requite thee* 6, 40; nuterá-ma (nu-ter-ra-am-ma) *we will restore* 4, 31.—(HW 701b)

tarçu (tarâçu *to stretch out*) properly *direction:* ana tarçi axâmiš *opposite one another* 3, r. 22.—(HW 715a)

Index of Proper Names.

א

E-ana (Assyr. Bît šame), *House of Heaven,* name of the temple of Ištar at Erech, 4, 3; 5, 3.

Uba'ânat (amel U-ba-a-a-na-at), a tribe dwelling on the western frontier of Elam, 1, 30.

Idû'a (I-du-u-a), servant of Kudurru, 5, r. 15.

Adi̯adî'a (Ad-i̯a-di-'a), a noble of the city of Irgidu and father of Dalân, **3**, 16.

Adar (DINGIR-BAR **14**, 5; **15**, 4) spouse of the goddess Gula; both deities often invoked by physicians, as patrons of the healing art.

E-zida (Assyr. Bîtu kenu) *The True Temple*, name of the temple of Nabû at Borsippa, **20**, 7.—(HW 323[a])

Akkadî, mât (KUR URI-KI) **4**, 29; **5**, 10, Babylonia.—Cf. Lehmann, *Šamaššumukîn*, i. p. 68 ff.

Ulâ'a (ID U-la-a-a), the river Eulæus (אולי, Εὐλαῖος), i. e. the modern Kerkha (against Delitzsch, *Paradies*, p. 329); see Johns Hopkins University Circulars, No. 114, p. 111[b]; cf. Part I. of this article (vol. xviii. p. 145, n. 1).

Elamtu, mât, Elam (עילם, 'Ελυμαία, 'Ελυμαίς), properly *Highland;* written KUR NIM-MA-KI, **1**, 9. 37. 39; **2**, 4. 17. 44; **3**, 9. r. 7. 15; **4**, 13; **5**, 9. 10. 14. 16. r. 10. 13.—Cf. Haupt, *Assyr. E-vowel*, p. 14 ff.; Delitzsch, *Paradies*, p. 320 ff.

Amedirra (A-me-dir-ra), an Elamite, father of the rebel Ummanigaš, **3**, r. 16.

Ummaxaldâšu, Ummanaldas, son of Attametu, king of Elam [Um-ma-xal-da]-a-šu, **2**, 5; Um-ma-xal-da-a-šu, **2**, 23. 34. 35. 58; **3**, r. 17; Um-ma-xal-da-šu, **3**, r. 20.—The name is written Um-man-al-da-si (var. das), KB. ii. **194**, 112; **196**, 2; Um-man-al-da-a-ši, ibid. **246**, 74; cf. also Xumba-xal-da-šu, ibid. **280**, 31. 33.

Umxulumâ' (Um-xu-lu-ma-'), an Elamite noble, **2**, 22. 46. 54.

Ammaladin (Am-ma-la-din), prince of I̯âši'an, **3**, 13.

Ummanigaš;—(1) king of Elam, son of Urtaku; Um-man-i-gaš, **6**, 9. 21.—(2) son of Amedirra, rebelled against Ummanaldas; Um-man-ni-gaš, **3**, r. 16.

Ummanšimaš (Um-man-ši-maš), an Elamite official (Nâgir), **2**, 11.

Undadu (Un-da-du), an Elamite official (zilliru), **2**, 11.

Upî'a (U-pi-a), Opis, a city at the junction of the Tigris with the Adhem, **18**, 12. r. 7.—Cf. Part I. of this article (vol. xviii. p. 171).

Iqîša-aplu (BA-ša-A), (*The god*) *has bestowed a son*, **3**, r. 10. 23.

Arba'il ([al]TATTAB-DINGIR), Arbela, properly *The city of the four gods*, **9**, 7; **10**, 7; **19**, 5.—(Delitzsch, *Par.* 124. 256)

Irgidu (Ir-gi-du), an Elamite city, two double leagues west of Susa, **3**, 11.

Arad-Ea (NITA-DINGIR-E-A), *Servant of Ea,* Assyrian priestly astrologer, **13**, 2.

Arad-Nanâ (NITA-DINGIR-Na-na-a), *Servant of Nanâ,* physician of Esarhaddon, **14**, 2; **15**, 2.

Uruk (Sumerian UNU-KI = Assyr. šubtu *abode*), the city of Erech (ארך), in Southern Babylonia; written UNU-KI **4**, 3. 5; **5**, 3. 5. 13. r. 8. 16.—(*Par.* 121 ff.)

Arapxa ([âl]Arap-xa), Arrapakhitis (Ἀρραπαχῖτις), a city and district, north of Assyria, about the sources of the Upper Zab, **18**, 12. r. 2. 11.—(*Par.* 124 ff.)

Išdî-Nabû (GIRI-DINGIR-PA), *Nabû is my foundation,* an Assyrian official, **10**, 2.

Ašur (properly *The Beneficent,* אשר), the national god of Assyria; written DINGIR-Ašur, **11**, 9; **17**, 6; Ašur (without DINGIR), **12**, 13; **18**, 4; DINGIR-DUG, **1**, 3; **2**, 2; **3**, 2; **6**, 12.—(HW 148[b])

Aššur, mât, Assyria (אשור); written KUR-Aššur-KI, **2**, 28; **3**, r. 4; KUR DINGIR-DUG-KI, **5**, 13.

Aššurû, Assyrian; pl. Aššure (DINGIR-DUG-KI-MEŠ), Assyrians, **6**, 34.

Ašur-mukîn-paléịa (Ašur-mu-kîn-BAL-ịa) *Ašur establishes my reign,* son of Sardanapallus, **12**, 10.

Ištar (*beneficent,* form Ⓠ[t] from אשר), the goddess Ištar; Ištar (DINGIR-NANNA) ša Uruk, **4**, 5; **5**, 5; Ištar (DINGIR-XV) ša Ninua, **9**, 6; **19**, 4; Ištar (DINGIR-XV) ša Arba'il, **9**, 7; **10**, 7; **19**, 5.

Ištar-dûrî (DINGIR-XV-du-ri), *Ištar is my wall,* an Assyrian official, **16**, 2.

ב

Bâbîlu, Babylon, properly *Gate of God;* Belit Bâbîli (KA-DINGIR-RA-KI), **19**, 3.

Bâbîlâ (KA-DINGIR-a-a), **17**, 4.—The name means *devoted to* (*the god of*) *Babylon.*—Cf. Part. I. of this article, p. 168.

Bâb-bitqi ([âl]KA-bit-qi), a city of Babylonia. Cf. Part I. p. 171.

Bel (*lord,* בעל), the god Bel; written DINGIR-EN, **2**, 39; **8**, r. 16; **9**, r. 9; **10**, 5; **17**, 7; **19**, 3; EN (without DINGIR), **12**, 13.

Bel-ibnî (DINGIR-EN-ib-ni), *Bel has begotten* (*a son*), an Assyrian general, and governor of the Gulf District, **1**, 2; **2**, 1; **3**, 2.—Cf. Part I. p. 134.

Bel-eṭer (DINGIR-EN-SUR), *Bel has preserved*, father of Pir'i-Bel, **5**, 7. 15.

Bel-upâq (DINGIR-EN-u-paq), *Bel gives heed*, writer of No. **20**, son of Kunâ, **20**, 1.

Bel-iqîša, *Bel has bestowed;*—(1) Prince of Gambûlu; DINGIR-EN-BA-ša, **4**, 12.—(2) One of the writers of No. **17**; EN-BA-ša, **17**, 3.

Balasî (Ba-la-si-i), Assyrian astrologer (Βέλεσυς), **12**, 3.

Belit (fem. cstr. of Bel), the goddess Belit; written DINGIR-NIN-LIL, **10**, 6; **18**, 4; DINGIR-NIN (Brünnow, No. 7336), **19**, 3; Belit (DINGIR-NIN) Bâbîli, **19**, 3.

Bît-Na'âlâni (E Na-a-a-la-ni), name of a district, **19**, 9.

ג

Gaxal (Ga-xal), grandfather of Šumâ, **1**, 7.

Gula (modification of GALA *great*), the goddess Gula, spouse of Adar q. v.; DINGIR Gu-la, **14**, 5; **15**, 5.

Gambûlu (ᵃˡGam-bu-lu), a district of Southern Babylonia, **4**, 9. 25.—(*Par.* 240 ff.)

ד

Daxxâ (ᵃᵐᵉˡDax-xa-'), an Elamite tribe, **1**, 10. 11.

Daxxadi'u'a (ᵃᵐᵉˡDax-xa-di-u-a), an Elamite tribe, **2**, 21.

Dalân (Dá-la-a-an), a noble of Irgidu, son of Adiadî'a, **3**, 15.

Deri (ᵃˡDi-ri), a city near the frontier of Elam and Babylon **16**, 18.—Cf. Part I. p. 165.

Dâru-šarru, *The king is eternal*, messenger of Nabû-ušabšî; Da-a-ru-LUGAL, **5**, 20; Da-ru-LUGAL, **5**, r. 23. 25.

Dûr-šarrukîn (ᵃˡBAD-DIŠ-MAN-GIN) *Sargonsburg*, a city of Assyria, north of Nineveh, **7**, r. 20.—Cf. Part I. p. 151.

ח

Xa'âdâlu ᵃˡXa-a-a-da-a-lu), a city in the highlands of Elam, **2**, 15; also called Xa'idâlu and Xîdâlu.—(*Par.* 328)

Xa'âdânu (ᵃˡXa-a-da-nu), a city of Elam, **3**, r. 19.—(*Par.* 329)

Xudxud (ⁿᵃʳXu-ud-xu-ud), a river in Elam, **3**, r. 18.—(*Par.* 329)

Xuxân (ᵃᵐᵉˡXu-xa-an), an Elamite tribe, **2**, 14.

ט

Ṭâb-çil-Ešára (DUG-GA-NUN-E-ŠAR-RA), *Good is the shelter of Ešára*, governor of the city of Aššur and eponym for the year 714 B.C., **18**, 2.—Cf. Part I. p. 171.

י

Iâši'an (^{amel}I̯a-a-ši-an), a district of Elam, 3, 14.

כ

Kidimuri, an Assyrian temple; Belit ^{ilat}belit Ki-di-mu-ri, 10, 6.—(HW 318^{a})

Kudurru (ŠA-DU), *Boundary*, governor of Erech, 5, r. 16.

Kalxu (^{al}Kal-xi), Calah (כלח), a city of Assyria lying a little south of Nineveh, 8, 7. 14.—(*Par.* 261)

Kunâ (Ku-na-a), father of Bel-upâq, 20, 2.

ל

Laxiru (^{al}La-xi-ru), a Babylonian city near the Elamite border, 3, 20.—(*Par.* 323)

מ

Madâktu (*camp*), an important city of Elam (Βαδάκη); ^{al}Ma-dak-tu, 2, 23; ^{al}Ma-dak-ti, 2, 7.—(*Par.* 325 ff.; cf. Haupt, in *Beitr. zur Assyr.* i. p. 171)

Marduk (DINGIR-MARADDA), Bel-Merodach, the national god of Babylon, 1, 3; 2, 2; 3, 2; 8, 5; 9, 5; 11, 3; 12, 7; 13, 5.

Marduk-erba (DINGIR-MARADDA-SU), *Marduk increase,* 19, r. 2. 6.

Mušêzib-Marduk (Mu-še-zib-DINGIR-MARADDA), *Marduk delivers*, nephew of Bel-ibnî, 3, r. 1. 6. 10.

נ

Nabû, Nebo (נבו), the special deity of Borsippa; written DINGIR-AK, 8, 5. 8. 9. 10. 12. r. 9. 16; 11, 3; 13, 5; 17, 7; 19, 4; 20, 4; DINGIR-PA, 9, 5. r. 9; 10, 5. r. 2; 12, 7.—Cf. Part I. p. 153.

Nabû'a (Na-bu-u-a), *Devoted to Nabû* (a name like Mar-dukâ, etc.), an Assyrian astrologer, 11, 2.

Nabû-axe-erba (DINGIR-PA-KUR-MEŠ-SU), *Nabû increase the brothers*, one of the writers of K. 565, 12, 4.

Nabû-erba (DINGIR-PA-SU), *Nabû increase,* an Assyrian physician, 16, 5.

Nabû-ušabšî, *Nabû has brought into existence,* an Assyrian official of Erech; written DINGIR-PA-GAL-ši, 4, 2; DINGIR-AK-GAL-ši, 5, 2.

Nabû-bel-šumâte (DINGIR-AK-EN-MU-MEŠ), *Nabû is the possessor of names* (i. e. many famous and honorable titles), the last Chaldean king of Bît-I̯akîn.—See the genealogical table below, p. 93.

Nabû-šum-iddina (DINGIR-PA-MU-AŠ), *Nabû has given a name.*—(1) An Assyrian priest, 8, 2; 9, 3.—(2) An Assyrian physician, 16, 4.

Nugû' (amel Nu-gu-u-'), an Elamite tribe dwelling near the Babylonian frontier, 3, 20.

Nadân (Na-dan), *gift*, a Chaldean of Puqûdu, 1, 17. 35.

Nanâ (DINGIR-Na-na-a), a Babylonian goddess, 4, 6; 5, 5; 20, 4.

Ninua (נינוה), Nineveh, the capital of Assyria; written Ninâ-KI, 9, 6; 19, 4; al Ninâ, 9, r. 6.—(*Par.* 260; cf. *Beitr. zur Assyr.* iii. p. 87 ff.)

Nin-gal (DINGIR-NIN-GAL), *Great Lady* (Assyr. beltu rabîtu), the spouse of the moon-god Sin, 13, 6. 9.

Nisxur-Bel (Nis-xur-DINGIR-EN), *Let us turn to Bel*, major-domo of Nabû-bel-šumâte, 2, 52.

Nusku (DINGIR-NUSKU), the Assyrian fire-god, 13, 6.

ס

Sallukkê'a (amel Sal-lu-uk-ki-e-a), an Elamite tribe, 2, 21. 50.

Sin (DINGIR-XXX), the moon-god, 12, 13; 13, 5. 9.

Sin-šarra-uçur (DINGIR-XXX-LUGAL-ŠEŠ), *O Sin, protect the king*, 6, 4.

Sin-tabnî-uçur (DINGER-XXX-tab-ni-ŠEŠ), *O Sin, protect (what) thou hast created*,[1] governor of Ur in Babylonia, 6, 1.

Sarâ'a (sal Sa-ra-a-a) writer of No. 19.—Cf. Part I. p. 173.

פ

Penzâ (al Pi-en-za-a), a city in or near the district of Tuškhan, 7, 9.—Cf. Part I. p. 151.

Puqûdu (פקוד, Ezek. xxiii. 23), a Chaldean tribe dwelling in Babylonia near the Elamite border; amel Pu-qu-du, 1, 18.—(*Par.* 240)

Pir'i-Bel (Pir'i-DINGIR-EN), *Offspring of Bêl*, son of Bel-eṭer, 5, 7; cf. note ad loc.

צ

Çabṭânu (al Çab-ṭa-nu), a city near the western frontier of Elam, 3, 7. 8.

---

[1] This explanation I owe to a personal communication from Dr. Bruno Meissner. I had rendered the name differently in Part I. p. 148, but Dr. Meissner's rendering seems preferable.

ר

Radê ([âl]Ra-di-e), a city of Elam, **2**, 49.—(*Par.* 327)

Rammân (DINGIR-IM), the god of the atmosphere (רמון), **12**, 14.

ש

Ša-Ašur-dubbu, governor of Tuškhan; written Ša-Ašur-du-bu, **7**, 2; Ša-Ašur-du-ub-bu, H. **139**, 2.—The word dubbu, which forms part of this name, would seem to be from the stem dabâbu *to speak.*

Šuxarisungur ([âl]Šu-xa-ri-su-un-gur) a city of Elam, **2**, 13; *Par.* 327 reads the final syllable si instead of gur.

Šumâ (Šu-ma-a), *My name,* nephew of Tammaritu, **1**, 6.

Šum-iddina (MU-SI-na), (*The god*) *has given a name,* father of Šumâ, **1**, 7.

Šamaš, the sun-god (שמש, شمس); DINGIR-BABBAR, **1**, 3; **2**, 2; **3**, 2; **4**, 16; **12**, 14; DINGIR-GIŠ-ŠIR, **6**, 8.

Šamaš-bel-uçur (DINGIR-BABBAR-EN-KUR), *O Šamas protect (my) lord,* Eponym for the year 710 B. C., **16**, 17.—Cf. Part I. p. 165.

Šupri'â ([mât]Šup-ri-a-a), the Suprian, **7**, 14. 19.—Cf. Part I. p. 151.

Šušan ([âl]Šu-ša-an), Susa (שושן), the capital of Elam, **3**, 13. —(*Par.* 326)

ת

Til . . ., a city on the frontier of Elam and Babylonia, **1**, 19.

Talax (Ta-la-ax), a city of Elam, **2**, 10. 49.—(*Par.* 327)

Tammaritu (Tam-ma-ri-ti), king of Elam, **1**, 8.—See genealogical table, p. 92)

Tâmti^{m}, mât (properly the *sea country;* cf. تهامة, the name of a sandy stretch of coast along the Red Sea), the Gulf District, i. e. the district lying about the shore of the Persian Gulf; mât Tam-tim, **3**, 5.—Cf. Haupt, in *Hebraica,* i. p. 220, n. 4.

Targibâti ([âl]Tar-gi-ba-a-ti), an Elamite city near the Babylonian frontier, **1**, 21.

Tašmetu^{m} (*intelligence,* properly *hearing*), a Babylonian goddess, spouse of Nabû; DINGIR-Taš-me-tum, **19**, 4.

- Šarru-kenu (Sargon), r. 722–705.
  - Sin-axe-erba (Sennacherib), r. 705–681.
    - [1] Ašur-nâdin-šum, King of Babylon 700–694.
    - Ašur-axa-iddin (Esarhaddon), r. 680–669; his mother was Nikâ.
      - Ašur-bân-apal (Sardanapallus), r. 669–626.
        - [6] Ašur-ctêl-ilâni, r. 626 —.
          - [8] Šerû'a-eṭerat, a daughter.
        - [7] Sin-šar-iškun (Sarakos), Succeeded his brother.
      - Šamaš-šum-ukin (Saosduchin), King of Babylon 668–647.
      - [3] Sin-iddin-apal
      - [4] Ašur-mukin-palê'a, High-priest of ......
      - [4] Ašur-etêl-šame-erçiti-balâṭ-su, High-priest of Sin.
      - [5] Serû'a-eṭerat, a daughter.
    - [2] Nergal-šar-uçur (Sharezer).
    - [2] Adar-mâlik (Adrammelech).

---

[1] *K. B.*, ii. p. 278, l. 30.

[2] Tiele, *Bab. Assyr. Geschichte*, pp. 309, 325; Adler, PAOS, Oct. '87, p. xxxiii.

[3] Knudtzon, *Gebete an den Sonnengott*, No. 107, 2. 7.

[4] Lehmann, *Šamaššumukîn*, Pt. I. p. 30; Pt. II, p. 20, ll. 12–13.

[5] Lehmann, o. c., Pt. II. p. 75; Harper's *Letters*, No. 113, rev. 8.

[6] *K. B.*, ii, p. 268.

[7] *Zeits. für Assyr.*, xi. p. 47.

[8] K 1619 b (Harper's *Letters*, No. 308), rev. 2–4; *J. H. U. Circ.*, vol. xv., No. 126, p. 91.

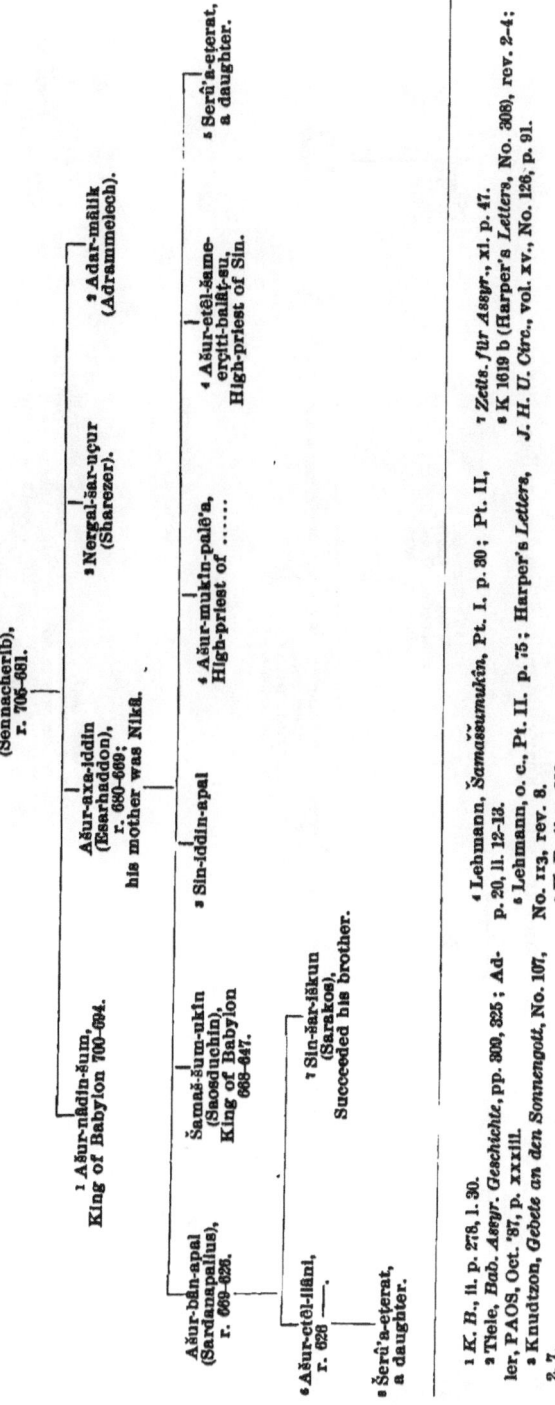

The Royal Family of Elam,

Contemporary with Esarhaddon and Sardanapallus.

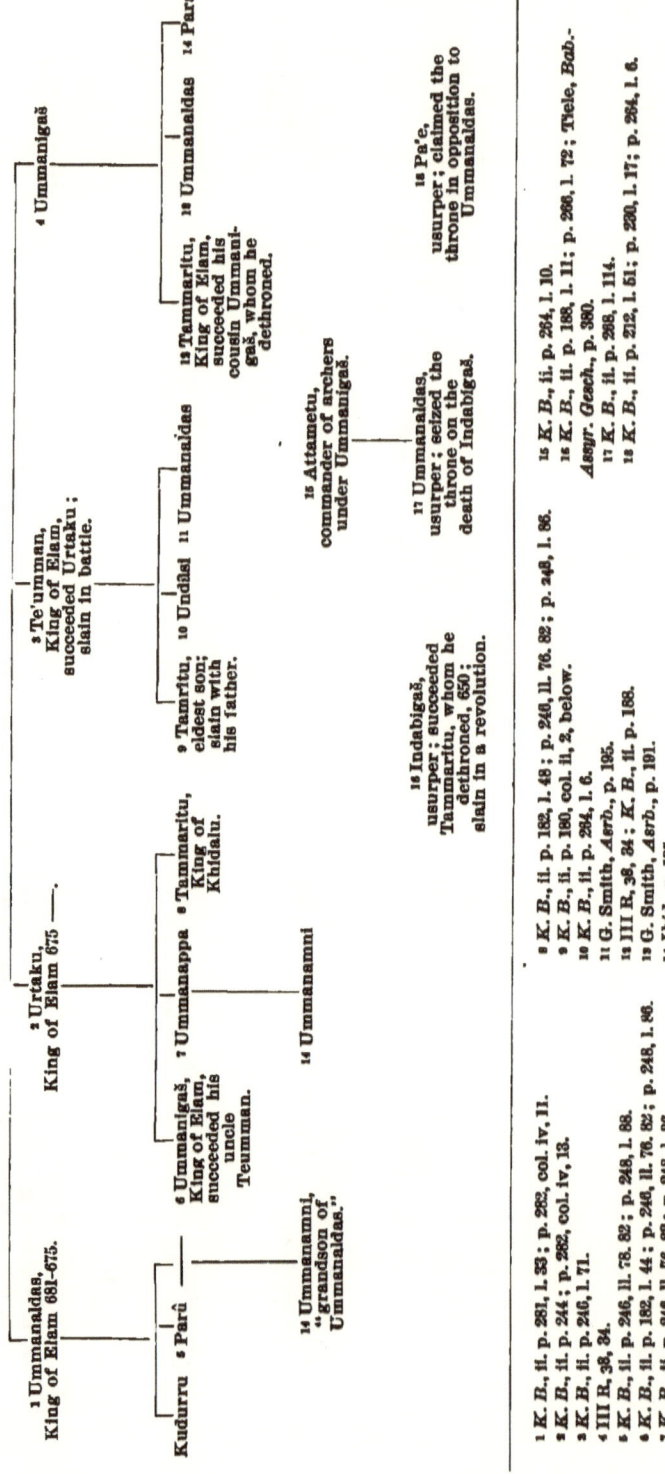

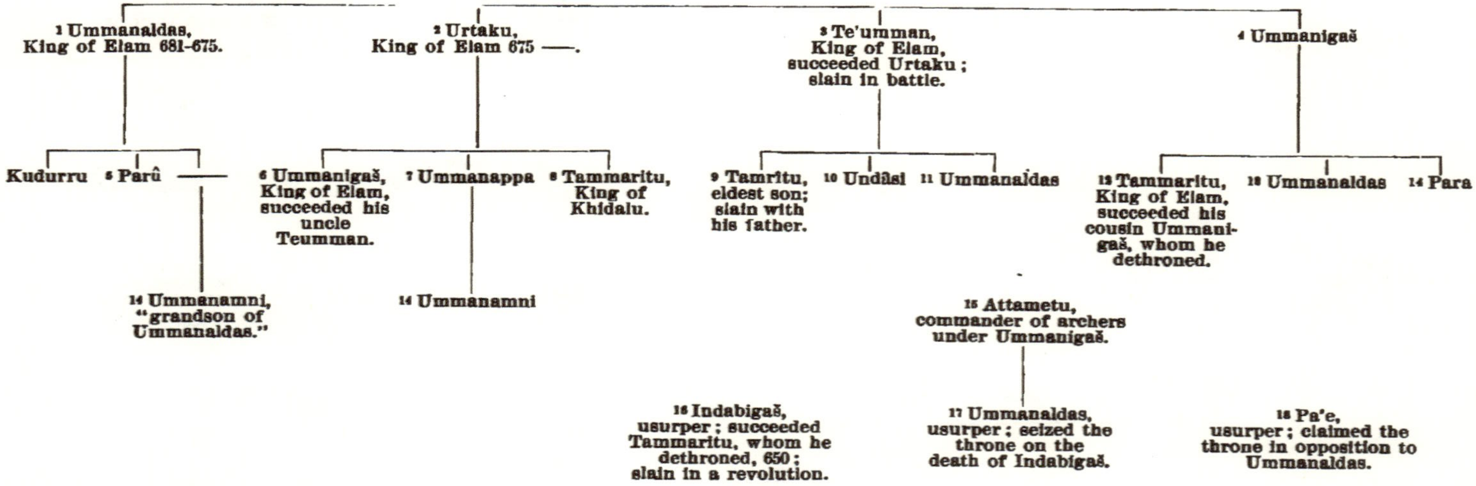

1 *K. B.*, ii. p. 281, l. 33; p. 282, col. iv, 11.
2 *K. B.*, ii. p. 244; p. 282, col. iv, 13.
3 *K. B.*, ii. p. 246, l. 71.
4 III R, 38, 34.
5 *K. B.*, ii. p. 246, ll. 78. 82; p. 248, l. 88.
6 *K. B.*, ii. p. 182, l. 44; p. 246, ll. 76. 82; p. 248, l. 86.
7 *K. B.*, ii. p. 246, ll. 76. 82; p. 248, l. 86.
8 *K. B.*, ii. p. 182, l. 48; p. 246, ll. 76. 82; p. 248, l. 86.
9 *K. B.*, ii. p. 180, col. ii, 2, below.
10 *K. B.*, ii. p. 264, l. 6.
11 G. Smith, *Asrb.*, p. 195.
12 III R, 38, 34; *K. B.*, ii. p. 188.
13 G. Smith, *Asrb.*, p. 191.
14 *Ibid.*, p. 195 [illegible]
15 *K. B.*, ii. p. 264, l. 10.
16 *K. B.*, ii. p. 188, l. 11; p. 266, l. 72; Tiele, *Bab.-Assyr. Gesch.*, p. 380.
17 *K. B.*, ii. p. 268, l. 114.
18 *K. B.*, ii. p. 212, l. 51; p. 230, l. 17; p. 264, l. 6.

THE CHALDEAN KINGS OF BÎT-IAKÎN.

[1] Marduk-apal-iddina (Merodach-baladan) of Bît-Iakin, King of Babylon 721–710, 703–702.

- [2] Nabû-šum-iškun, captured at the battle of Khalule, 692.
- [3] Nabû-zer-lišir, King of the Gulf District, slain in Elam, 680.
- [4] Na'id-Marduk, King of the Gulf District, 680.
- Nabû-salim
  - [5] Aplâ, surrendered to Sardanapallus by Ummanigaš King of Elam.
- Nabû-apal-iddina
  - [6] Nabû-bel-šumâte, King of the Gulf District; rebelled against Sardanapallus, and was finally, at his own command, slain in Elam by his armor-bearer.

---

[1] *K. B.*, ii. p. 14, l. 26; p. 276.

[2] *K. B.*, ii. p. 108, col. vi, 6.

[3] Also called Nabû-zer-napišti-lišir, and Zer-keniš-lišir; *K. B.*, ii. p. 128, l. 32; p. 144, l. 15; p. 282, l. 39.

[4] *K. B.*, ii. p. 128, l. 35; p. 144, l. 20.

[5] *K. B.*, ii. p. 256, l. 65; Smith *Asrb.*, p. 135, l. 61.

[6] *K. B.*, ii. p. 212, l. 28; p. 266.

N. B.—Cf. Winckler's article "Die Stellung der Chaldäer in der Geschichte," published in his *Untersuchungen*, p. 47–64.

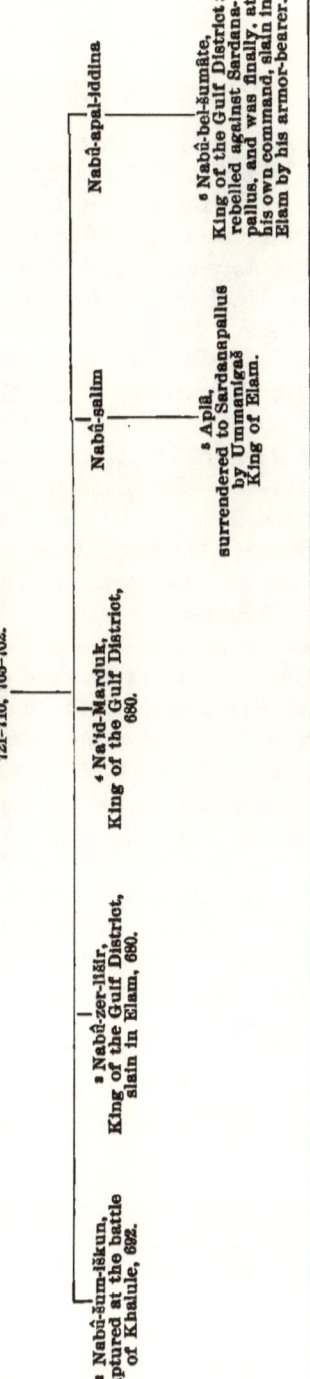

Bibliography.

As the literature of the subject is not extensive, I have endeavored to give here a complete bibliography of all works dealing especially with Assyrian Letters. It has not, however, been thought necessary to notice all epistolary texts incidentally published or translated in Assyriological publications. For these see Part I. pp. 125–129, Dr. Berry's paper noticed below, and Bezold's *Catalogue of the K. Collection.*

Amiaud, Arthur, *Esarhaddon II.* Babylonian and Oriental Record, ii. pp. 197 ff. Translation of K.1619[b], with historical and philological notes.

Berry, George Ricker, *The Letters of the R^M 2 Collection.* Hebraica, xi. pp. 174–202.—Introduction (174–178) containing full bibliography; fourteen texts in transliteration (178–183); notes (183–193); glossary (193–202), but without translations.

Delitzsch, Friedrich, *Beiträge zur Erklärung der babylonisch-assyrischen Brieflitteratur* (three papers). Beitr. zur Assyr. i. pp. 185–248 (list p. 327); 613–631; ii. pp. 19–62.—Forty texts in transliteration, with translations and explanatory notes.

Harper, Robert Francis, *Assyrian and Babylonian Letters belonging to the K. Collection of the British Museum.* Vols. i. (1892), ii. (1893), iii. (1896), iv. (1896).—Containing in all 435 letters, not only from the K. Collection, but also from the other Collections of the British Museum.

———. *The Letters from the R^M 2 Collection.* Zeits. für Assyr., viii. pp. 341–359.—The Assyrian texts of fourteen letters.

——— *Assyriological Notes.* I. Hebraica, x. pp. 196–201; II. Am. Journ. Sem. Lang., xiii. pp. 209–212; III. *Ibid.*, xiv. pp. 1–16.—These articles contain chiefly lexicographical material derived from the Letters.

Johns, Rev. C. H. W., *Sennacherib's Letters to his father Sargon.* Proc. Soc. Bib. Arch., xvii. pp. 220–239.—Transliteration and translation of K. 181, K. 5464, K. 125, with notes; text of R^m *2* II. 14.

Johnston, Christopher, *Two Assyrian Letters.* Jour. Am. Or. Soc., xv. (1892), pp. 311–316.—K. 84 and K. 828 in transliteration, with translations and notes.

——— *Note on K. 84.* Johns Hopkins University Circulars, xii. No. 106 (June 1893), p. 108.

Johnston, Christopher, *Assyrian Medicine.* Johns Hopkins University Circulars, xiii. No. 114 (June 1894), pp. 118–119. Contains translation of S. 1064.

——— *The Epistolary Literature of the Assyrians.—Ibid.*, xiii. No. 114 (July 1894), pp. 119 ff.

——— *The Letter of an Assyrian Princess. Ibid.*, xv. No. 126 (June 1896), pp. 91 ff.—Contains translation of K. 1619[b], with historical introduction and notes.

Lehmann, C. F., *Zwei Erlasse Königs Asurbanapals.* Zeits. für Assyr., ii. (1887), pp. 58–68.—Text, transliteration, and translation of K. 95 and 67, 4–2, 1, with notes.

Meissner, Bruno, *Altbabylonische Briefe.* Beitr. zur. Assyr., ii. pp. 557–572; 573–579.—Text, transliteration, and translation of V. A. Th. 809, 574, 575, 793, with notes.

Pinches, Theo. G., *Notes upon the Assyrian Report Tablets.* Trans. Soc. Bib. Arch., vi. (1878), pp. 209–243.—Treats K. 181, K. 528, K. 79, K. 14. General Introduction (209–313); summary of contents of the four letters (213–219); text, transliteration, translation, and notes, 220–243.

——— *Assyrian Report Tablets.* Records of the Past, xi. (1878), pp. 75–78.—Translations of K. 493, K. 538, K. 11, K. 562.

——— Transliterations and translations of 89, 7–19, 25, and 80, 7–19, 26.—Proc. Soc. Bib. Arch., Nov. 1881, pp. 12–15.

——— *Zwei Assyrische Briefe übersetzt und erklärt.* Leipzig (Pfeiffer), 1887.—S. 1064 and K. 824; cf. S. A. Smith's *Keilschrifttexte Asurbanapals*, vol. ii., pp. iv., 58–67.

——— *An Assyrian letter anent the transport, by ship, of stone for a winged bull and colossus.* Bab. and Or. Rec., i. 1886–87), pp. 40–41; 43–44.—Text, transliteration, and translation of S. 1031, with notes.

——— *Specimens of Assyrian Correspondence.*—Records of the Past (2[d] series), ii. (1889), pp. 178–189.—Translations of S. 1064, K. 538, K. 84.

Smith, Samuel Alden, *Keilschrifttexte Asurbanipals*, Leipzig (Pfeiffer), 1887–89.—Vols. ii. (1887) and iii. (1889) contain text, transliteration, and translation of thirty-five letters, with notes by the author and additional notes by Pinches, Strassmaier, and Bezold.

——— *Assyrian Letters.* Proc. Soc. Bib. Arch., ix. pp. 240–256; x. pp. 60–72; 155–177; 305–315. Reprinted separately, under the same title, 1888.—Text, transliteration, and translation of thirty-three letters, with notes.

Talbot, H. Fox, *Defense of a Magistrate falsely accused.* Trans. Soc. Bib. Arch., vi. pp. 289–304.—Text, transliteration, and translation of K. 31, with brief notes. The translation is reproduced in Records of the Past, xi. (1878), pp. 99–104.

List of Abbreviations.

AJSL : *American Journal of the Semitic Languages.*
APR : Meissner, *Beiträge zum altbabylonischen Privatrecht.*
BA : *Beiträge zur Assyriologie und vergleichenden semitischen Sprachwissenschaft* (Delitzsch and Haupt).
H : Harper's *Assyrian and Babylonian Letters.* Texts are cited by number, not by page.
HW : Delitzsch, *Assyrisches Handwörterbuch.*
JHU Circ.: Johns Hopkins University Circulars.
KB: Schrader, *Keilinschriftliche Bibliothek.*
PAOS: *Proceedings of the American Oriental Society.*
PSBA : *Proceedings of the Society of Biblical Archæology.*
Par.: Delitzsch, *Wo lag das Paradies?*
SK.: Winckler, *Sammlung von Keilschrifttexten.*
Str. Nbk.: Strassmaier, *Inschriften von Nabuchodonosor.*
Str. Nbn.: Strassmaier, *Inschriften von Nabonidus.*
T^c: Tallqvist, *Sprache der Contracte Nabû-nâ'ids.*
TSBA : *Transactions of the Society of Biblical Archæology.*
W: Delitzsch, *Assyrisches Wörterbuch.*
ZA: *Zeitschrift für Assyriologie.*

Numbers in heavy-faced type, not otherwise qualified, refer to the texts treated in Part I. of this article. For example, **17**, 2, refers to No. **17** (Part I., p. 169), line 2 ; **8**, r. 6 = No. **8** (Part I., p. 155), reverse, line 6.

§ refers to the paragraphs in Delitzsch's *Assyrian Grammar.*

The verbal stems are designated as follows :—𝔔 = Qal, 𝔔^t = Ifteal = Piel, 𝔔^{tn} = Iftaneal, 𝔑 = Nifal, 𝔑^t = Ittafal, 𝔍 (Intensive), 𝔍^t = Iltaal, 𝔖 = Shafel, 𝔖^t = Ishtafal.

Other abbreviations used require no explanation.

VITA.

I was born in Baltimore on the 8th of December, 1856, the eldest son of Dr. Christopher Johnston, Professor of Surgery at the University of Maryland. Having received my preparatory training in private schools, I matriculated in October, 1872, at the University of Virginia, where, after having pursued the full curriculum of that institution, I received the degree of Master of Arts in July, 1879. During the sessions of 1877–78 and 1878–79 I also followed medical courses. In 1880 I was graduated as Doctor of Medicine by the University of Maryland. While practicing medicine in Baltimore from 1880 till 1888, I devoted nearly all my spare time to the study of ancient and modern languages. In October, 1888, I entered the Johns Hopkins University as a special student; was appointed, in the following year, Fellow in Semitic, being reappointed in 1890. In November, 1890, I was appointed Instructor in Semitic. I received the degree of Doctor of Philosophy from the Johns Hopkins University in 1894, and in the same year was appointed Associate.

While a student in the University I attended the courses of Prof. Haupt, Prof. Gildersleeve, and Dr. Adler. I desire to offer my thanks to all my instructors, and especially to Prof. Haupt, to whose friendly aid and counsel I owe more than I can well express.

www.ingramcontent.com/pod-product-compliance
Lightning Source LLC
Chambersburg PA
CBHW032111010726
47493CB00008B/2545
* 9 7 8 3 3 3 7 2 3 5 6 7 3 *